Enjoy all of these American Girl Mysteries®:

THE SILENT STRANGER   A *Kaya* Mystery

LADY MARGARET'S GHOST   A *Felicity* Mystery

SECRETS IN THE HILLS   A *Josefina* Mystery

THE RUNAWAY FRIEND   A *Kirsten* Mystery

SHADOWS ON SOCIETY HILL   An *Addy* Mystery

THE CRY OF THE LOON   A *Samantha* Mystery

SECRETS AT CAMP NOKOMIS   A *Rebecca* Mystery

A THIEF IN THE THEATER   A *Kit* Mystery

CLUES IN THE SHADOWS   A *Molly* Mystery

THE PUZZLE OF THE PAPER DAUGHTER   A *Julie* Mystery

and many more!

D0109634

— A *Kit* MYSTERY —

MISSING
GRACE

by Elizabeth McDavid Jones

★ AmericanGirl®

Published by American Girl Publishing, Inc.
Copyright © 2010 by American Girl, LLC

Questions or comments? Call 1-800-845-0005, visit our
Web site at **americangirl.com**, or write to Customer Service,
American Girl, 8400 Fairway Place, Middleton, WI 53562-0497.

Printed in China
10 11 12 13 14 15 LEO 10 9 8 7 6 5 4 3 2 1

PICTURE CREDITS
The following individuals and organizations have generously
given permission to reprint illustrations contained in "Looking Back":
pp. 174–175—dog show, Morgan/Hulton Archive/Getty Images;
Bouvier girls with white terrier, © Bettmann/Corbis; pp. 176–177—
Depression-era family, © Bettmann/Corbis; puppy, © Fancy/Veer/Corbis;
Rin Tin Tin poster, ON THE BORDER © Turner Entertainment Co.
A Warner Bros. Entertainment Company. All rights reserved;
pp. 178–179—poodles with trainers, Morgan/Hulton Archive/Getty Images;
registration papers, American Kennel Club archive collection; basset hound,
Clary/AFP/Getty Images; pp. 180–181—prize ribbon, American Kennel Club
archive collection; Westminster Dog Show, © Bettmann/Corbis;
TIME magazine cover, reprinted through the courtesy of the Editors of
TIME Magazine, © 2009 Time Inc.; modern girl with dog, Cultura.

Illustrations by Jean-Paul Tibbles

Cataloging-in-Publication Data available from the Library of Congress

To my husband, Rick—
life partner, friend, father of my children

Without his support and long hours of
child care, this book could not have been written.

TABLE OF CONTENTS

1
CELEBRITY DOG

"This has to be the hottest day we've had all summer," declared Kit Kittredge. Kit and her friends Stirling Howard and Ruthie Smithens were perched in the glider swing under an oak tree in Kit's front yard. On the table beside the swing sat three almost-empty glasses of iced tea—iced tea that hadn't cooled Kit and her friends down one bit in the stifling heat of the August afternoon.

Kit's basset hound, Grace, was sprawled in the shade at Kit's feet, asleep. Grace's short legs were splayed out flat underneath her long body. Stirling's face was buried in the morning newspaper, the *Cincinnati Register*. Kit and Ruthie had been reading library books, but now they were using the books as fans.

"It's too hot to do anything," Ruthie agreed. "Even read."

"I feel like one of Mother's petunias over there—wilted," Kit said. She jutted her chin toward the drooping flowers lining the flagstone walkway that led from Kit's front steps to the street. Then Kit's gaze went to the roof of the house, where the chimney's blackened stones reminded her of the disaster that had nearly befallen her family a few weeks earlier.

The fire. Kit still felt a twist of fear whenever she thought about the fire, so she did her best not to think about it. She jerked her eyes away from the roof, back to Grace. Grace had waked up long enough to stretch luxuriously. Then she rolled onto her side and closed her eyes again.

"I feel wilted, too," said Ruthie. "It must be a hundred degrees."

"The paper says it's only going to be ninety-five today," corrected Stirling, peering at the weather forecast.

Stirling and his mother boarded with the Kittredges. When Kit's dad lost his job because of the Depression, Kit's family had rented out some of their bedrooms to help pay their bills. The Howards slept in Kit's old room, and Kit slept in the attic now. The other boarder, Mr. Peck, slept in Kit's brother Charlie's old room, since Charlie had a job out west for the summer. There were usually boarders staying in the guest room, too, but they had moved out before the fire.

Which was a good thing—what Kit's mother called *providential*—because the guest room had been damaged by the smoke.

"Of course," Stirling was going on, "tomorrow it's going to be hotter—ninety-eight degrees." He began reading aloud from the newspaper. "'The summer of 1935 has seen record-breaking high temperatures. And more are yet to come.'"

Suddenly he stopped reading and pointed to something in the newspaper. "Look, Kit!" He held up the Letters to the Editor section for Kit and Ruthie to see. "More letters responding to the column you wrote about Grace saving us from the fire. See? 'Heartwarming Feature,'

3

this one says. And look at the title of this letter:
'Celebrity Dog'."

As Kit took the paper to read the letters, a
shiver went down her spine. *The night of the fire.*
It seemed unreal now: the thunderstorm, the
power going off, her family and the boarders
spending the evening in front of the fireplace
roasting hot dogs for supper. And later, Grace
nudging Kit awake in the middle of the night
with her cold nose and pushing her head up
under Kit's arm, so that Kit couldn't go back
to sleep.

Then Kit had smelled the smoky haze drift-
ing through her attic bedroom and had seen
a yellowish, flickering light outside. Kit had
leaped from her bed, rushed to the window, and
seen flames flashing up from the chimney and
a black column of smoke billowing above.

Now, looking back, Kit remembered the rest
of that night as separated moments frozen in
her brain, like a series of snapshots in a photo
album: hurrying down the stairs with Grace,
waking up her parents and the boarders, seeing

the out-of-control fire raging in the fireplace and the heavy, choking smoke billowing into the living room, and then all of them—Kit, her family, Grace, and the boarders—stumbling outside into fresh air—and safety.

Soon the fire trucks had arrived, and the fire had been put out. Luckily, the fire itself had remained inside the chimney. Smoke had damaged the living room and the guest room—the rooms next to the chimney—but, thanks to Grace, everyone had escaped the fire unhurt.

Kit had written about Grace and the fire in the children's column she'd been writing for the *Cincinnati Register* as a summer job. The newspaper had printed the column alongside a picture of Grace and Kit in front of their house, with a caption underneath that told how Kit had found Grace abandoned two years ago and taken her home. Since Kit's article had come out, people had been writing letters to the newspaper, saying how much they'd enjoyed reading about Grace's heroic deed.

Grace had become a celebrity. Neighborhood

kids came in droves to play with her, people walking past the house stopped and stared if Grace was in the yard, and strangers rang the doorbell and asked to see her.

That morning a woman with a carload of kids had come by and asked if she could take the children's picture with Grace. Then the children had begged to stay and play with Grace. Grace had chased balls and been chased herself, played hide-and-seek, and endured petting and poking, ear tugging and tail pulling. As soon as the children left, Grace had plopped down in the shade, and she hadn't budged since.

Kit's thoughts snapped back to the present when Grace gave a sudden snore so loud, it made Kit jump. Ruthie and Stirling jumped, too. They all laughed so hard, they had to hold their stomachs. When Kit could stop laughing long enough to talk, she said, "Poor Grace! Being Celebrity Dog must have worn her out."

"I guess it takes a lot of energy to be a star," said Stirling.

"Especially in *this* heat," Ruthie added.

"Yeah," Kit agreed, putting the newspaper on the table beside her. "The heat sucks the energy right out of you like a vacuum cleaner. *Burrr-burrr.*" Imitating a vacuum cleaner, Kit reached over and started tickling Ruthie. Ruthie broke into loud giggles.

Then they heard voices from the front porch. Kit looked up. Mother had walked out on the porch with a tall, thin woman wearing a business suit. The woman had gray hair pulled back in a bun and a crabby expression on her face.

Oh, no, thought Kit. *That woman must be the potential boarder Mother said she was going to interview today.* Kit couldn't help wishing Mother would turn the woman down.

"Who's that?" whispered Ruthie.

"Her name is Miss McLenny," said Kit in a low voice. "She *might* be our new boarder."

"I hope not," said Stirling. "She looks as sour as a lemon. And I'll bet she snores, too— as loudly as Grace."

"If we don't rent out the guest room soon," Kit said, "we won't be able to make the payments

on the chimney repair and the new furniture
Dad and Mother had to buy after the fire. And
Miss McLenny is the only person who answered
Mother's ad for a boarder in the *Register*."

"When would you like to move in?" Kit
heard Mother say. Kit groaned. It sounded as
if Mother had already rented the room to Miss
McLenny.

"The sooner the better," Miss McLenny
replied. "As long as you take care of the *dog
problem*."

"Tomorrow is Friday," Mother said. "Would
that suit you?"

"I'll have my things delivered in the morning," said Miss McLenny.

"Good," Mother answered with a smile.
"We'll be looking forward to getting to know
you." She held out a friendly hand to Miss
McLenny.

Miss McLenny didn't lift her own hand to
take Mother's. "I doubt there will be time for
us to get to know each other, Mrs. Kittredge.
I shan't be staying more than a few weeks. Just

until I can find something more permanent, you understand."

Mother, looking a bit taken aback, withdrew her hand. "Why, yes, you mentioned that. Shall I call you a cab? We don't have a telephone, but I could go next door and—"

"Thank you, no," Miss McLenny interrupted, in a voice as crisp as stale toast. "The proximity of your house to the bus stop is the only reason that I've chosen to board in a house with children and a . . . *dog*."

Then, tossing a sour look toward Kit and her friends, Miss McLenny marched past them, her high-heeled shoes *click-clicking* on the flagstone walk. At the mailbox, Miss McLenny turned onto the main sidewalk and *click-clicked* up the street.

Mother walked from the porch to the swing where Kit and her friends were sitting. "Well, children," she said, "at last we have a new boarder." Mother didn't look very happy about it, and Kit didn't blame her one bit.

"Mother, what did Miss McLenny mean by

the *dog problem*?" Kit asked.

"Oh, you heard that," said Mother. She sighed. "Miss McLenny, it seems, isn't too fond of children, and she *detests* dogs. She refused to rent the room unless I promised that Grace would sleep outside."

"But Mother!" Kit said. "Grace wouldn't bother *her*! Grace sleeps up in the attic with me."

"I told Miss McLenny that," Mother said. "But she insisted that was her condition for taking the room. As you know, we're in no position to be overly choosy about our boarders."

"It doesn't seem fair," Kit said, "to repay Grace for what she did for us by making her sleep *outside*."

Mother brushed a hand against Kit's cheek. "I know how you feel, Kit, but it's only temporary, until Miss McLenny finds an apartment downtown closer to her new job. And it *is* summertime, after all. Grace will be fine sleeping on the back porch for a few weeks. Try to understand, won't you?"

On the inside, Kit felt angry and upset that

Mother had agreed to banish Grace from the house, but she tried not to let it show on the outside. Kit knew that she wasn't the only one who had to make sacrifices because of the Depression. She gave Mother as much of a smile as she could muster and nodded.

After Mother had gone back into the house, Kit jumped off the swing and sat cross-legged beside Grace. Affectionately, she ruffled the fur on Grace's neck. "Oh, Gracie, *I* might understand, but will you?"

Grace opened her eyes and thumped her tail. Then she lifted her big head, laid it in Kit's lap, and made a rumbling sound deep in her throat. It was the sound she always made when she was trying to tell Kit something.

Ruthie slid off the swing and sat on the ground with Kit and Grace. "See? That's her answer, Kit. She *does* understand." Ruthie scratched Grace behind one of her long, floppy ears.

Kit nuzzled her face into the softness of Grace's neck. "Whoever said dogs can't talk?"

"Obviously someone who never had a dog," Stirling said. He sat down on the ground beside Grace and the girls. "It won't be that bad for her to sleep outside, Kit. It'll be harder on you than on Grace."

"But she's not *used* to being outside at night," Kit worried. "What if she's scared of the dark?"

"Grace?" said Stirling. "Celebrity Dog? *She's* not afraid of anything." He stroked the short fur on Grace's back.

Then Ruthie said, "Uh-oh, Kit, look who's coming this way." She pointed to two boys a few houses down walking barefoot along the sidewalk. "Roger. And he has *Butch* with him."

Roger was a bully in Kit's neighborhood and in her class at school, and Butch was his best friend. They both loved playing mean tricks and making fun of people, especially Kit and Stirling.

Kit groaned. "What do *they* want?"

"To pester us, I'm sure," said Stirling.

"Let's just ignore them," Ruthie suggested.

"Maybe they'll leave us alone."

"Fat chance of that," Kit grumbled. "But we'll try it."

Kit turned away from Roger and Butch and stroked Grace. Ruthie and Stirling turned away, too, acting as if something intensely interesting was happening at the other end of the block.

Then Stirling whistled. "Forget Roger," he said. "Look at that car! Have you ever seen such a beaut?"

Kit looked up to see a large, fancy Cadillac driving slowly down the street. It was a light cream color with black fenders, whitewall tires, and a shiny hood ornament on the front. The closer the car got to Kit's house, the slower it went, until it came almost to a standstill in front of Kit's mailbox.

"Must be more of Grace's admirers trying to get a glimpse of her," Ruthie commented.

"At least it's not a carload this time," Stirling added.

"Yeah," Kit said. "Looks like only three people in the car." Besides the driver, a man wearing a fedora-style hat with a feather, there was another man in the passenger seat and a boy in the back. "And lucky for Grace," Kit added, "only *one* of them is a kid." Kit, Ruthie, and Stirling chuckled.

Grace, as if she knew she was being discussed, cocked her head and gazed curiously at the Cadillac.

At the same time, the man in the passenger seat of the car leaned forward to look in Grace's direction. Kit grinned at him and waved. The man just looked away, and the car sped off.

"Goodness," said Kit, "*they* weren't very friendly."

"You probably embarrassed them," said Stirling. "I'll bet they didn't want us to notice them staring at Grace."

"What makes you think they were staring at your stupid hound anyway?" It was Roger. Kit had momentarily forgotten him and Butch.

The two bullies were standing on the sidewalk on the other side of the hedge that separated Kit's yard from her neighbor's. They laughed and pointed at Grace. "Nobody rich enough to own a Cadillac would look twice at that mutt," Roger taunted. "She's so ordinary, she makes a bucket of mud look special."

"Yeah," Butch said, snickering. "And she's so clumsy, I bet she can't walk without tripping over those dopey long ears."

Grace was wagging her tail at the boys, but they just laughed at her. It made Kit so mad, she felt like she was about to boil over. Roger's making fun of *her* was one thing, but making fun of Grace wasn't fair. Grace loved everybody, and she thought the boys' laughing meant they wanted to play.

Kit thought of a hundred angry things she wanted to say to Butch and Roger, but she held the words back. Instead she gave the bullies an icy stare. Stirling and Ruthie were glaring at them, too, but neither Kit, Ruthie, nor Stirling spoke a word.

At first, it seemed that not answering the bullies back was going to work. With loud chortles, Butch and Roger started to walk away.

Their bare feet slapped against the sidewalk
as they sauntered past Kit's house, snickering
at Grace. They went on past two more houses.
Then they turned around. Roger, cupping his
hands around his mouth, called loudly, "I'm
disappointed, Kit. I read in the paper about your
celebrity dog, so I wanted to come see it."

"We thought you'd gotten a *new* dog," Butch
threw in. "A *special* dog."

"But I should have known better," Roger
said. "I should've remembered that your family
is *too poor* to buy a dog—or anything else!"

Kit leaped up with an angry reply, but the
bullies were already hurrying away. She could
hear them laughing all the way down the street.

2
A FINICKY BOARDER

Friday morning Miss McLenny moved in, and her complaints began. She insisted that the bedroom furniture be dusted, even though it was brand-new, because dust made her sneeze. The bedsheets had to be re-laundered, because sheets that weren't fresh enough made her itch. And the rugs on the floor had to be taken outside and aired, because musty smells would give her a headache.

It was Kit who had to do the dusting, laundering, and airing. The whole time she worked, Kit grumbled to herself about the headache Miss McLenny's complaints were giving *her.*

When Miss McLenny finally pronounced the room acceptable and disappeared inside, Kit breathed a sigh of relief. Of course, by then it was almost dinnertime, and Kit had to help Mother prepare the meal for seven people. After dinner, Miss McLenny was the only one who didn't help with the cleanup. Kit couldn't help hoping that Miss McLenny would find a new, more permanent place to live very soon.

That night, Kit fixed a cozy box for Grace on the back porch, with Grace's favorite blanket and the chew toy Kit had made for her from braids of rope knotted together. Grace jumped right into the box and lay down to gnaw on the toy.

This is going to be easier than I imagined, Kit thought.

Problem was, Grace didn't seem to understand that she was supposed to *sleep* in the box. The minute Kit opened the back door to go in, Grace hopped up and was at Kit's side, ready to follow her.

"No, Grace," Kit said. "You stay here. This is where you're sleeping tonight." Grace looked up at Kit and thumped her tail against Kit's legs, but she didn't budge.

A FINICKY BOARDER

Kit gave Grace a gentle push away from the door. "Stay here, Grace," Kit said more firmly. Grace didn't stay. She stepped toward Kit so that she was between Kit's legs and looked up again, with a determined expression. *I go where you go,* the look seemed to say.

The look nearly broke Kit's heart, but she had no choice. She had to get Grace to stay out on the porch. "No, Grace!" Kit said sharply. "Stay!" Then she pushed Grace away and slipped through the door into the kitchen. Kit braced her back against the kitchen door and squeezed her eyes shut. She hated doing this to Grace!

Grace gave a few short barks. She started scratching at the door and whining in the most pitiful way. Kit couldn't bear to listen, but neither could she bring herself to go out of the room and leave Grace alone in her misery. Kit slumped down at the kitchen table and tried to keep from crying. She felt like such a traitor! If only she could explain to Grace about finicky boarders and mortgage payments . . .

Grace kept on whining and scratching, and

Kit kept sitting at the table. She watched the hands on the kitchen clock creep to nine and then to nine-thirty. Mother came in to check on Kit, and so did Dad. They agreed that it would be okay for Kit to stay up until Grace settled down.

Finally Grace was quiet. Kit stood up and turned off the light. She pulled back the curtain that covered the window of the kitchen door and peered out. Nothing stirred on the dark porch. The only sound was the light patter of rain on the roof and the faraway moan of a train whistle.

Kit was overwhelmed with loneliness. This was the first night Grace hadn't slept at Kit's side since Kit and Stirling had found her abandoned on the sidewalk. Grace had had a sign around her neck that said, *Can't feed her any more.* She had been Kit's constant companion ever since.

A tear slid down Kit's cheek. Quickly she swiped it away with the back of her hand. *No use crying over what can't be helped,* she told herself. She pressed her palms against the door.

"Good night, Gracie," she whispered. Then she went up to bed. But it was a long time before she fell asleep.

In the morning, Kit awoke to the smell of pancakes cooking. *Saturday morning,* her sleepy brain told her. *Dad's up early to make breakfast for the boarders so that Mother can sleep a little later.* Drowsily Kit slid her hand off the bed to be licked by Grace. It was their wake-up ritual. Grace always gave Kit's fingers a good-morning lick, and Kit gave Grace a good-morning scratch under the chin.

Then Kit remembered that Grace wasn't *here.* She had slept outside on the porch. Instantly Kit was wide-awake. She *had* to say good morning to Grace and reassure her that Kit still loved her. Kit jumped out of bed, threw on her clothes and sneakers, and raced down the attic stairs.

All was quiet in the upstairs hall. Mr. Peck's room was empty—he was an early riser—but the other bedroom doors were still closed, and Kit tiptoed past them. She couldn't help snickering when she heard loud snores coming from behind Miss McLenny's door. *If Miss McLenny could hear herself snore,* Kit thought, *she would probably complain about **that**, too.*

Quietly Kit flew downstairs to the living room. Mr. Peck was sitting on the new sofa Kit's parents had bought after the fire, reading the newspaper. "Good morning, Mr. Peck," Kit said as she rushed through the room.

Mr. Peck looked up. "Good morning, Kit. You're up early. And in a hurry, I see."

"Checking on Grace," she explained.

Kit hurried into the kitchen. Dad was at the stove, pouring pancake batter onto the griddle. "Whoa, Nellie!" Dad said. "How's my Cub Reporter this morning?"

That was Dad's pet name for Kit, because Kit wanted to be a reporter. Also because Kit liked to type up her own newspapers and pass them out to family and friends. She always kept a little black notebook and a pencil in her pocket, so that she could jot down anything she thought was newsworthy.

"Racing off to cover a story?" Dad teased. "Or do you have time for a kiss for the pancake chef?"

"Always time for you, Dad." Kit kissed his cheek. "How's Grace this morning?"

"Since she's not at the door demanding a pancake," Dad said with a grin, "I imagine she's still asleep."

"She slept better than I did, then," Kit said.

"Miss her?" Dad flipped a pancake.

Kit nodded. Dad, spatula in one hand and a pot holder in the other, planted a kiss on Kit's head. "It won't be for long."

"I hope not. Need any help?"

"These pancakes are for Mr. Peck," said Dad. "Later, when everyone else eats, you can set the table. For now, tend to Grace. After last night, she'll be wanting lots of extra attention, I expect."

"Grace *always* wants attention," Kit said.

"And *food*," Dad added with a twinkle in his

eye. "Don't dare go out there without Grace's breakfast."

"Oh, yes! Thanks for reminding me." Kit grabbed the bag of dog food from the pantry; Grace's dish was already outside. Then Kit pulled open the door to the porch, bracing herself for Grace to come barreling at her and jump all over her, the way Grace usually greeted her whenever they'd been apart. But Grace didn't come.

Shutting the kitchen door behind herself, Kit stepped onto the porch. She didn't see Grace anywhere. Then Kit's eyes fell on the hook that latched the screen door shut.

The hook was hanging loose, unfastened.

A sick feeling came over Kit. She'd been so upset about leaving Grace on the porch, she must have forgotten to fasten the hook. Grace must have pushed the screen door open and gone out. Since the door opened outward, she wouldn't have been able to get back in.

A lump came to Kit's throat. Poor Grace! Trapped outside in last night's rain. Kit pictured

Grace, wet and miserable, huddled under the back porch all night.

Maybe she's there now, Kit thought.

Kit hurried down the steps and jumped over a muddy patch at the bottom. She stooped and peered into the shadows under the porch, calling Grace's name. But no happy yip greeted her.

Kit straightened. Shielding her eyes from the sun, Kit scanned the backyard and out by the garage and chicken coop. The chickens were up, clucking and scratching, but Grace was nowhere to be seen. Kit studied the patchwork of backyards, flower beds, and patios in both directions. No Grace.

"Grace!" Kit called as loudly as she could. "Come, Grace!" She waited, hoping to see a familiar streak of brown-and-black-and-white dog come charging around someone's house toward her. But Grace didn't appear. Then Kit trotted around to the front yard and called Grace again. Grace didn't show.

Worry clenched Kit's insides. *Where was Grace?*

Kit walked slowly around the house to the back-porch steps and started to go up. Then she spied part of a footprint in the mud at the base of the steps. It couldn't have been Kit's print; she had leaped *over* the mud. Besides, the print had been made by a bare foot, and Kit was wearing sneakers. There was a clear impression of five bare toes pressed into the mud—kid-sized toes. But the heel hadn't made a print. It looked like someone had walked on tiptoe up to the porch.

Kit lifted her head, puzzling over the footprint. Her eyes landed on the screen door. Just above her head, a small section of screen was loose from its wooden frame, as if someone had pushed in the edge of the screen and then tried to tuck it back into place. Someone who had wanted to reach inside to unlatch the door and let a dog off the porch ...

Grace didn't wander away on her own, thought Kit. *Someone took her!*

3
THE BULLIES' PRANK

The first two "someones" who burst into Kit's mind were Roger and Butch.

Fury rose in Kit. It would be just like those two to steal Grace in order to play a mean trick on Kit. And they had both been barefoot on Thursday!

Kit raced up the steps, across the porch, and through the kitchen door. Mother was at the table, having coffee with Dad. Mr. Peck was there, too, eating his pancakes.

"*There* you are," Mother said. "We were wondering what had happened to you and Grace." Then Mother's face clouded. "What's wrong, Kit?"

"Is something wrong with Grace?" Dad asked.

"Yes, where is she?" Mr. Peck said.

Kit told them about Grace's disappearance, the pushed-in screen and the footprint, and her suspicion about Butch and Roger. The adults agreed that it sounded as if the bullies had played a nasty prank on Kit.

"They might've taken Grace off somewhere and set her loose to find her way home," said Dad.

"Wait an hour or two," suggested Mother. "Grace may wander home. If not, you and Stirling may need to go out and find her."

After breakfast, Grace still hadn't returned, so Kit and Stirling set out to look for her. "Let's get Ruthie," said Kit. Ruthie lived on the street behind Kit. Over the years, the girls had worn a path between Kit's backyard and Ruthie's.

At Ruthie's house, her aunt Nancy answered the door. Aunt Nancy was Mr. Smithens's younger sister. She'd taken a vacation from her work to stay with Ruthie while Ruthie's parents were on a trip. Nancy was single, drove a convertible car with a rumble seat, lived in an apartment building downtown, and had a job in a big department store.

Aunt Nancy greeted Kit and Stirling. "Ruthie and I were squeezing lemons to make lemonade. Would you like to help?"

Kit explained that Grace had disappeared and that they wanted Ruthie's help searching for her. Aunt Nancy said Ruthie could go with them.

The threesome started off in the direction of Roger's house. It was already getting hot, but the streets were cooled by the trees' sun-dappled shade. Kit and her friends walked past brick and wood-frame houses to hilly Berkshire Drive, where they saw old Mrs. Cox on her front porch.

The friends decided to ask Mrs. Cox if she knew anything about Grace. They trooped up her steps. Kit told her why they had come and described Grace to her.

"Since you sit out on your porch so much," said Stirling, "we were hoping you might have seen Grace come by."

"It would've been early this morning," added Ruthie.

"Hmm." Mrs. Cox put a finger to her cheek. "I might've seen that dog. With a long body? She stands about this high?" She held a wrinkled hand two feet off the ground.

"Yes!" Kit said. "Yes!" She could hardly contain her excitement.

Mrs. Cox bobbed her chin. "I saw her, all right. A boy had her on a rope, the two of 'em trotting along the sidewalk as fast as they both could go."

The three friends looked at each other. "Did you recognize the boy?" Kit asked. "Was it Roger from down the street?"

Mrs. Cox cackled, as if Kit had told her the funniest joke she'd ever heard. "Oh, my land. With these old eyes, I couldn't tell you who the boy was. I'm doing well to tell the boy from the dog. Oh, dearie me." She took off her glasses and wiped tears of laughter from her eyes.

After the friends left Mrs. Cox, they gathered on the sidewalk. "It must have been Roger!" Kit said. "Or Butch. You know how often Butch sleeps over at Roger's house."

"Maybe it was *both*," said Stirling. "With her bad eyesight, Mrs. Cox might have missed one of them."

"Whichever it was," said Kit, "I want to know where they were headed with Grace."

"Probably to Roger's house," suggested Ruthie.

"No," said Stirling, "Roger would figure his house would be the first place we'd look for Grace."

Kit nodded. "Where else would he have taken her?"

"They like to ride bikes to Mount Storm Park," Ruthie said. "They might've gone there and set Grace loose. Then it would take her a while to find her way back home."

"And in the meantime, I'd be worried sick about her!" said Kit. "That does sound like Roger!"

"Then let's go talk to him," said Stirling.

It was two more blocks to Roger's house. Kit rang the doorbell. Inside she heard the blare of a radio. When Roger's mother answered the door, Kit asked if Roger could come out.

His mother looked worried. "Is anything the matter, Kit? Has Roger done something?" She knew that Roger and Kit didn't get along, and that it was mostly Roger's fault.

"Well—" Kit began. Then someone shut off the radio, and Roger appeared behind his mother.

"Roger," said his mother in a firm voice, "go outside and talk to Kit. And whatever you've done, tell her you're sorry."

"Aw, Ma," he said, "I haven't done anything to her."

His mother stared down her nose at him. "Let's hope not," she said and went back inside the house.

Roger stepped onto the front stoop and closed the door behind him. He gave Kit, Ruthie, and Stirling a scornful look. "What do you jokers want? And where's that mangy hound you always have with you?"

"That's what we came over to ask *you*," said Stirling.

"We know what you and Butch did," said Ruthie. "And we won't tell your mother if you admit it and tell us where Grace is now."

"Yeah, what did you and Butch do with my dog?" Kit demanded.

"Oho," Roger said. "Don't tell me your celebrity dog is *missing*."

"Don't pretend you don't know what we're talking about, Roger," Kit said hotly. She'd been hoping Roger would just confess that he'd played a mean trick and tell her where Grace was. But she should have known better.

"If you'll just tell us where Grace is—" Ruthie began.

"Did you and Butch dump Grace off at Mount Storm Park?" Stirling asked.

Roger got an evil gleam in his eyes. "Wouldn't you love to know?"

Frustration welled up inside Kit. *Roger isn't going to tell us what he did with Grace...* Tears were prickling behind Kit's eyelids. She blinked them away. All she wanted to do was get Grace back. She didn't even care about getting Roger into trouble for what he'd done.

"Look, Roger," said Kit. "*Please* tell us if you took Grace to the park. It's *blocks* from here. I'm not sure she could get back home by herself." Kit stopped. Her voice was trembling, and she was afraid she was going to cry.

Roger's expression softened. "Don't go blubbering about it, Kit. If your dog wandered off, she can find her way home. She's a hound dog, isn't she? They're supposed to be good with their noses." His tone became jeering again. "And she's *special,* remember?"

Then hurriedly he added, "I gotta go. We're going someplace." With that he opened the door, slipped into the house, and closed the door in Kit's face.

"Ring the bell again, Kit," Ruthie urged, "and this time tell his mother what he did. She'll make him tell us the truth."

Kit wiped tears from her eyes. How embarrassing to get emotional in front of Roger! "No," she said. The last thing she wanted was for Roger's mother to see her crying, too. "You heard him. He practically admitted they took Grace to the park. Let's go and look for her there."

"It's not going to be easy," warned Stirling. "With all those woods and the lake and the walking trails and ball fields, she could be *anywhere*."

"And rabbits and squirrels to chase, and kids to play with on the playground," Ruthie added.

"If Grace is there," said Kit with determination, "we'll find her."

Kit, Ruthie, and Stirling combed every inch of the park. They called Grace until they were hoarse. They asked people all over the park if they'd seen her. On one of the walking trails, they met a man walking a male basset hound on a leash. Kit introduced herself, told the man where she lived, and explained what had happened to Grace. She asked him if he had seen a female basset hound at the park, wandering around loose.

"No," said the man, "I would've noticed

another basset hound, and Roland here *certainly* would have noticed. He's always in the mood to meet other bassets, especially a good-looking female." He told them his name was Mr. Panetta and he lived on Hedgerow Place, not far from Kit. "Perhaps we could let our basset hounds get acquainted sometime," he suggested.

"Of course," Kit agreed. "Grace loves to meet other dogs, too. But first we have to find her."

Mr. Panetta wished them luck and walked on. Kit, Ruthie, and Stirling kept looking for Grace and asking people about her. At last, a woman with a baby in a carriage who was watching her older kids on the playground said she *had* seen a dog that looked like Grace.

"I was here early this morning," she said, "taking baby Jenny for a stroll before breakfast." The baby stirred from sleep and whimpered, and the woman placed a pacifier in her mouth. "A boy about your age was sitting on that bench over there, with a basset hound on a rope." She nodded toward a wooden bench nearby.

Kit's eyes flicked to the bench and back.

"Only one boy? What did he look like?"

"Did he have brown hair or blond?" Stirling asked. Roger had brown hair and Butch was blond.

"Blond," the woman replied without hesitation. "So blond it was almost white. And he was barefoot."

"Butch!" Kit, Stirling, and Ruthie said together.

The woman smiled. "A friend of yours?"

"Not exactly a *friend*," said Ruthie.

"Did you see what he did with the dog?" Kit asked. "Did he let her loose?"

The woman shook her head. "I couldn't tell you that. We walked past and then went home."

The three friends thanked the woman and left the playground.

"Now we're getting somewhere," said Kit. "We know for sure that Butch took Grace and brought her here to the park."

"And Roger was probably in on it, too," Ruthie suggested.

Kit bit her lip, thinking hard. "I wonder if he

was. I found only *one* footprint. Mrs. Cox saw *one* boy with Grace. And so did that woman—a blond-headed boy, so it had to have been Butch. But I do think Roger knows where Grace is. He knows what Butch did with her."

"I think so, too!" Stirling exclaimed.

"We looked all over the park," said Ruthie. "Grace isn't *here.*"

"Maybe Butch changed his mind about turning her loose and decided to *keep* her," Kit said. "Why else would he be sitting on a park bench with her? If he'd planned to turn her loose, he would've just *done* it."

"It's hard for me to picture Butch being that softhearted," said Stirling.

Kit doubled her hands into fists. "What we need to do is go back to Roger's house and make him tell us the *truth.* If Butch did take her home, then Roger had better tell us where Butch lives so we can go get her. And if Butch did something else with her, Roger had better tell us that, too."

4
PRIME SUSPECT

The heat was going out of the afternoon as Kit, Ruthie, and Stirling walked the long blocks back to Roger's. No one was home. "We'll try again later," Kit decided.

After dinner, the trio returned, and lights were on inside the house. Kit rang the doorbell. "I'm coming!" called a young female voice. Then Elaine, Roger's older sister, opened the door. She was home from college for the summer.

Kit asked for Roger, but Elaine told them her parents had left that morning to take Roger to summer camp. "He'll be gone for a solid week, and I plan to enjoy every minute without him here to pester me."

Kit groaned. "A whole week! But we need to ask him what Butch did with Grace!" She explained their ideas about Butch and Roger's prank.

"Those stinkers!" said Elaine. "I wouldn't be surprised if Butch *did* take Grace home with him. It sounds like something he would do."

Kit asked Elaine if she knew where Butch lived. "Or even his last name. Then we could look up his address in the phone book."

"All I know is his last name—Johnson," Elaine replied. "Whenever Roger has Butch over, I try to stay away from them. Roger's bad enough alone, but together they are *sooo* annoying." She rolled her eyes.

After thanking Elaine, the friends started home through the falling dusk. Fireflies winked in the pockets of darkness under trees and around shrubs. "Tomorrow's Sunday," said Ruthie. "If you and Stirling come over after lunch, we can call every Johnson in the phone book until we find Butch."

When Kit and Stirling walked over the next day, Ruthie was waiting for them on her patio. A police car was parked in the driveway behind Aunt Nancy's convertible. "Why are the police at your house?" Stirling asked Ruthie.

Ruthie laughed. "Aunt Nancy's fiancé, Paul, is visiting. He's a police sergeant, so he's allowed to drive the squad car home. We'll go in the back door so we won't disturb them."

The friends settled down in Ruthie's den with the phone book, but they found pages and pages of Johnsons listed. Ruthie heaved a frustrated sigh. "It would take us days to call all these numbers."

"I'd be willing to call every single one to find Grace," declared Kit.

"There must be a better way of tracking Butch down," said Stirling.

At that moment Aunt Nancy came into the den and asked Ruthie what they were doing. Ruthie explained about trying to find Butch among all the Johnsons in the phone book.

"Hmm," said Aunt Nancy, "almost like

trying to find a missing person. Maybe Paul could help. The police have cases like that a lot."

"Please ask him!" begged Ruthie.

Aunt Nancy called Paul into the den, and Kit, Ruthie, and Stirling told them both everything that had happened. "It's so frustrating," Kit said. "All of our clues point to Butch as the one who took Grace."

"But we can't get Grace back," said Ruthie, "because we don't know where Butch lives."

"And Roger's away at summer camp for a week, so he can't tell us," Stirling added.

"Ah," said Sergeant Paul with a smile, "you need more information about your prime suspect."

"Yes!" Kit exclaimed. "How do the police go about it when they're trying to solve a crime?"

"In much the same way you're doing," said Sergeant Paul. "Searching out clues, following up every possibility, noticing things that are out of the ordinary, gathering information and keeping careful track of it all. That's how our detectives work."

"Kit has a notebook where she writes *everything* down," Stirling announced.

"And she's great at noticing unusual things," Ruthie threw in. "She's been writing a children's news column all summer for the *Register*."

"It's a very good column," said Aunt Nancy. "I read it every week."

Sergeant Paul raised his eyebrows. "So you're a budding reporter, Kit."

Kit felt the heat of embarrassment on her cheeks. "I'd like to be a reporter when I grow up, anyway."

"You're off to a good start," Sergeant Paul said. "And it sounds as if you already have the skills you need to crack this case."

"I hope so," said Kit.

Then Sergeant Paul scratched his head. "I wonder..." he said. He told them about some recent dog thefts in the city. "The story was in this morning's newspaper. The stolen dogs were both valuable show dogs—and both basset hounds. One of the thefts happened yesterday in broad daylight."

"Do you think the thefts might be related to Grace's disappearance?" Aunt Nancy asked Paul.

"What do you think, Kit?" asked Sergeant Paul. "Are you sure this boy Butch took Grace?"

"A kid took Grace, not a dog thief," Kit said. "The footprint we found was too small to belong to an adult."

"You may be right," said Sergeant Paul. "I'd like to see this notebook of yours, Kit. Do you have it with you?"

"She *always* has it with her," said Ruthie.

Kit told Sergeant Paul she hadn't started taking notes yet about Grace's disappearance. "I thought it was only a prank and Grace would soon be home."

"Wouldn't it be a good idea to start now?" Sergeant Paul asked.

"Yes!" Kit declared. She pulled her notebook and pencil out of the back pocket of her overalls.

"We'll help you think, Kit," said Ruthie. "Maybe all of us together can figure out a way to get Grace back right away."

"Do you mind if Paul and I listen in?" asked Aunt Nancy.

"Of course not," said Kit. "And we'd appreciate any help you could give us." She chewed on the end of the pencil. "Maybe we should start with our witnesses—the people who saw Grace after Butch took her."

"Mrs. Cox and the woman at the park," said Stirling.

"Two witnesses." Kit opened her notebook and wrote **Witnesses** at the top of a page. Under that she wrote:

> Witness One. Mrs. Cox saw a boy early Saturday morning leading a basset hound on a rope. The boy seemed to be in a hurry.
> Witness Two. Woman at Mount Storm Park saw a blond, barefoot boy (Butch?) with a basset hound on a rope, before breakfast Saturday morning.

"I guess it's possible that the boy at the park might not have been Butch," suggested

Ruthie, "and the dog might not have been Grace."

Kit titled another page **Possibilities.** Under that she wrote: Boy at park not Butch, basset hound at park not Grace.

"Good point, Ruthie," Sergeant Paul said. "When the police are working on a case, they try to keep an open mind about their clues. Sometimes things aren't what they seem."

"Someone who saw Grace at the park might have thought that she was a stray or that she'd been abandoned," said Stirling, "and they might have taken her home."

"That's a good point, too," Aunt Nancy said.

Kit added to the **Possibilities** page: Grace mistaken for stray or abandoned pet. Then she looked up from writing. "*I* still think Butch took Grace."

"He does seem to be your most likely suspect," agreed Sergeant Paul. "Maybe you should make a list of everything Butch might have done with her."

Kit turned the page in her notebook. "I'll

need lots of space for that." She wrote in big, bold letters: **BUTCH: What did he do with Grace?**

The friends told Nancy and Paul the ideas they'd already considered on their own—that Butch had either set Grace loose at the park or taken her home to keep as his own pet. Kit wrote both of those down.

"Good, good," said Sergeant Paul. "Keep thinking. Spit out every thought that comes to you."

"Well," Kit began slowly, "there's a pet store in the Clifton business district, near the park. What if Butch took Grace there and tried to sell her to the store?"

"I bet Butch would be just mean enough to do that!" Ruthie burst out.

"I don't know." A crease showed on Aunt Nancy's forehead. "With so many pets being abandoned, would a pet-store owner be interested in buying an ordinary hound like Grace?"

"Remember, Nancy," said Sergeant Paul, "we're considering *every* possibility. If Grace is a particularly nice-looking dog, it's conceivable that a pet-store owner might be interested in her."

"Grace is the prettiest basset hound you've ever seen," Kit declared.

"Basset hounds do have a certain appeal," agreed Sergeant Paul, "with those big sad eyes and long floppy ears."

Aunt Nancy laughed. "I see what you mean. They are lovable dogs."

"And Grace is the *most* lovable of all," said Kit.

"Then write your idea down, Kit," Aunt Nancy suggested. Everyone waited while Kit wrote on the **Butch** page: Sold Grace to a pet store.

They thought a little longer but couldn't come up with any other ideas. "Which lead would you say is your strongest?" Sergeant Paul asked Kit. "You should follow up on that one first."

"Going to Butch's house to see if he took Grace home," said Kit. "But first we have to find out where he lives."

"We can talk to Roger's mother," Stirling offered, "and see what she can tell us about Butch."

"Roger's parents are bound to come home tonight," Ruthie said. "They both have jobs, so they'll have to be at work tomorrow."

"Let's try to catch Roger's mother in the morning before she leaves for work," Kit suggested.

"What about your other leads?" Sergeant Paul glanced at Kit's list of possibilities. "How about the stray dog idea? How will you follow up on that?"

Stirling's eyes were bright. "We could put a lost-dog ad in the paper."

"I know!" Kit exclaimed. "Maybe Mr. Gibson would let me do one more column for the *Register.*" Mr. Gibson—or Gibb, as all the reporters called him—was the editor of the newspaper, and he had hired Kit to write a children's column for the summer. "'Celebrity Dog Goes Missing' could be the headline. More people would see that, and it wouldn't cost us anything."

"That's a great idea!" said Ruthie and Stirling. Sergeant Paul and Aunt Nancy thought so, too.

In her notebook, Kit started a fresh page with **Our Investigation** at the top and wrote down what everyone had suggested. Then she closed her notebook.

"I'll write the column for the newspaper tonight," said Kit, "and we can go to the *Register* office tomorrow to take it to Mr. Gibson. I'm sure he'll be willing to print it if I keep it short. On the way home, we can stop at the Clifton pet store and check for Grace there."

5

A PECULIAR FAMILY

The next day, Mother gave Kit permission to skip her morning chores so that she and Stirling could talk to Roger's mother and take Kit's column to Gibb at the *Register*. "If you need to," Mother said, "spend the rest of the day looking for Grace. I'll feed the chickens, and weeding the garden can wait until tomorrow. This house doesn't seem right without Grace around."

Mother asked only that Kit be home in time to help her prepare an early dinner. "Dad and I are going to a meeting. And Mr. Peck has an evening orchestra rehearsal."

Kit grinned and gave Mother a hug. "Thank you, Mother."

Kit and Stirling rushed off to Roger's house. Elaine answered the door. She was still in her pajamas. "Both Mom and Dad have already left for work," she said, "but Mom's usually home by four-thirty. Try back then, Kit. I'll leave her a note to tell her you'll be by."

After leaving Roger's, Kit and Stirling went to pick up Ruthie, and the three of them headed downtown to the *Register* office. They had to wait almost an hour to see Gibb, but he told Kit he'd be happy to print her column about Grace's disappearance.

"It's short," he said. "I think we can fit it in tomorrow's edition. And I hope it helps you get her back." He pulled a pencil from behind his ear. "Tell me your phone number. I'll add it to the article so that people can call you if they have information about Grace."

Kit felt her face flame with embarrassment. She hated telling people her family couldn't afford a telephone. "We don't ... have a phone."

"Don't worry about that," said Gibb. "People can call the newspaper and talk to my secretary, Miss Preston. In a few days, you can come back and see if anyone's responded. Now, if you kids will excuse me, I have to get to a meeting."

The friends left Gibb's office and hurried down the stairs, talking excitedly about the possibility of finding Grace at the pet store near Mount Storm Park.

It was a long walk from downtown, but at last they were standing in front of the pet store. *Pets Galore* was painted on the window. Underneath, a smaller sign said: *Everything You Need for Your Dog or Cat.* Kit opened the door and went in, her stomach fluttering with nervous anticipation. Stirling and Ruthie were right behind her.

The store was noisy with the sounds of animals—barking dogs, meowing kittens, squawking parrots. There was a glass case with gerbils and pet mice, and one with a big green lizard. One wall had nothing but fish aquariums with brightly colored fish. On two walls were animal pens holding cats and dogs, kittens and puppies. One glance at the animals in the pens told Kit that Grace wasn't here. *At least not now,* she thought.

A man came from behind the counter and said, "May I help you kids with something?"

Stirling stepped forward. "We're looking for a basset hound."

"I don't have any basset hounds at the moment," said the man. "But I can sell you a fine-looking poodle. Or how about an adorable cocker spaniel puppy?"

"No," Kit said, "we're looking for a *missing* basset hound."

"Kit's basset hound, Grace, disappeared on Saturday," Ruthie explained. "And later someone saw her at the park."

"We wondered if someone might have brought Grace here to try to sell her," Stirling added.

"I have been known to buy grown dogs occasionally," said the man, "if it's a popular breed I think I can sell in the store. No one's brought in a dog to sell recently, though. But, you know . . ."

The man wrinkled his forehead and then began to nod. "A boy did come in here with a basset hound on Saturday. Said he'd just gotten the dog."

"Was the boy blond-headed?" Kit's heart had begun to thump.

"Can't say as I remember the color of his hair. Could have been blond. I dunno. I remember he had his parents with him, though."

"His *parents?*" Ruthie said.

"Yep," said the man. "The father bought supplies—a collar and leash, dog food, the sort of thing you buy for a new pet."

"What did the basset hound look like?" Kit asked.

"A real fine-looking female," said the man. "Quality animal. That's why I remember thinking it was all a little odd."

"Odd?" Kit said quickly. "In what way?"

The owner scratched behind his ear and seemed reluctant to answer Kit's question. Now Kit was *really* curious.

"To tell the truth," the owner finally said, "the family was dressed right shabbily. They looked like they hadn't had enough to eat in a while, either. Which is a shame, because the woman was expecting a baby. She must've been eight months along. Had this terrible, hacking cough, too. I felt right sorry for her."

The man paused and raised his hands, palms upward, in a gesture that said he couldn't make sense of the people's actions. "Yet here they were, spending money on this hound... and the hound looked better off than they did. They were a peculiar family, all right."

"How could a family like that afford to feed a dog?" Stirling asked.

"The father paid me for his purchases with good money," said the pet man. "That's all I care about."

Kit was confused. *A peculiar family with a fine-looking basset hound.* Grace was fine-looking, but the boy didn't sound like Butch at all. Butch had a hefty build, and he always had nice clothes.

"Please, mister," Kit said, "I really want to find my dog. I'm wondering if this family might have her. Is there anything about them you can remember that might help me find them?"

The man gave Kit a long look; Kit could tell he felt sorry for her. Then he said, "The parents spoke with a real strong foreign accent. German, I think."

Kit pressed her lips together in frustration. There was a huge German community in Cincinnati. Stirling must have been thinking the same thing. "There are so many Germans here, mister," he said. "Isn't there *anything* else you could tell us?"

"Did they say where they lived?" Kit asked. "Or what their names were?"

The pet man sighed. "Look, kids. When customers come into my store, they want to buy pets or pet supplies, and it's my job to sell to them. I don't ask a lot of questions. Sometimes customers talk to me; sometimes they don't. The family with the basset hound was in and out in a few minutes. They barely spoke. But tell you what I'll do. If they come back in, I'll try to find out more and give you a call."

Ruthie gave him her number, and the friends

left the store. When they were out on the sidewalk, Ruthie said, "I don't think that dog could have been Grace, do you, Kit?"

"Sergeant Paul told us to follow up every possibility," Kit reminded her. "And I intend to do just that. Maybe Butch set Grace loose at the park, and this boy found her. We need to track down his family and get a look at their basset hound. Who knows? It *might* be Grace. It sounds as if the family got their dog the day Grace disappeared."

"How do we even begin to look for them?" Stirling asked. "All we know is that they *might* be German, and they *might* have a blondheaded son. It'll be like looking for a needle in a haystack."

Kit screwed up her mouth, thinking. "Maybe not. What about the soup kitchen? If the family didn't have enough to eat, that's where they'd go to get a meal."

"And the soup kitchen workers might remember them," said Stirling.

Ruthie pulled some coins out of her pocket

and counted them. "I've got just enough money for streetcar fare for the three of us to get to the soup kitchen, but we'd have to walk home. What do you think? Should we go now?"

"Let's," said Kit.

"We'd better get going," Stirling announced. "From downtown, it'll take a long time to walk home."

Soon Kit, Ruthie, and Stirling were on the orange streetcar, headed for the River Street stop, which was only a block from the soup kitchen. While they were riding, Kit brought her notebook up to date. She wrote down:

Witness Three. Pet-store man saw blond-headed (maybe) boy with a basset hound in pet store on Saturday morning. Boy was with his parents (German? Not enough to eat? Poor. Mother has bad cough, expecting a baby very soon). Called this family "peculiar." Said basset hound was "fine-looking female. Quality animal."

On the **Possibilities** page she wrote: Peculiar family might have Grace. (Did boy find Grace at park?) Under **Our Investigation**, she wrote: Go to soup kitchen and see if anyone there knows where to find family from pet store.

When the trolley lurched to a stop at River Street, the friends got off and walked to the soup kitchen. It was mid-afternoon, so the place was quiet. The workers were preparing vegetable soup for the evening meal. Kit recognized the director, a gray-haired woman wearing a hairnet, who was chopping vegetables at a counter. Kit asked her if she had time to talk to them about a family who might have visited the soup kitchen.

The director smiled and said she'd be glad to help them. Kit described the strange family to the director and told her why she wanted to find them.

"Do you remember seeing a family like that eating here?" Ruthie asked.

"Why, yes," the director said. "You're talking about the Muellers, I'm certain. They've been living at the hobo jungle for the last few months and coming here every day to eat. Until about a week ago."

"What happened then?" asked Stirling.

The woman pursed her lips. "We're not sure. Most of our regulars will tell us if their circumstances change so that they won't be coming back. They may have gotten a job, or found a place to live, or decided to move on somewhere else. It's true that Mr. Mueller struggles with speaking English, but he understands it well enough, and he can speak enough to get his meaning across most of the time. Yet the Muellers never said a word about not returning. They just stopped coming."

"You have no idea why?" asked Kit.

The director shook her head. "We've been concerned about them because Mrs. Mueller was ill, and she was due to have her baby soon. Mr. Mueller had been trying to find odd jobs to earn money to take her to the doctor, but he hadn't been able to find any work. We'd all been hoping he would find something soon, so he could get some housing for his family. That hobo camp is no place to birth a baby."

Kit nodded in agreement. She'd been to the hobo jungle to visit her friend Will. It was near the train station, under a trestle bridge that spanned the Ohio River. The jungle wasn't much more than a muddy patch cleared of brush along the riverbank, where hoboes who rode the rails in search of work camped out. Some of the hoboes were families like the Muellers, with children, even infants. Most had no shelter from the weather except an old, worn tent or a tumble-down shanty fashioned from cast-off boards. It would be a dismal place to have a baby.

"Perhaps Mr. Mueller found a job at last," the director went on, "and that's why his family hasn't come back. We can only hope. I'm sorry that I can't be more helpful, Kit. Do you really think the Muellers might have your dog?"

"We don't know, ma'am," said Kit. "We're just looking everywhere we can to find her."

"Good luck," said the director.

The friends left the soup kitchen and walked

down the street to the drugstore. They sat on a bench outside under the store's orange and blue Rexall sign while Kit wrote in her notebook. She started a new page and titled it The Muellers. Underneath she wrote: Where do we find them?

Slowly Kit closed the notebook and leaned forward to brace her elbows on her knees. Her head had begun to throb. She rubbed her temples, discouragement brimming up in her. "How do we even begin looking for the Muellers? If they've stopped coming to the soup kitchen, they must not be living at the hobo jungle anymore."

"The hoboes are all friends," said Stirling. "Maybe the other hoboes could tell us where the Muellers went."

Kit sat up straight, her spirits instantly lifted. "Great idea, Stirling!" She flipped her notebook open again to Our Investigation and wrote: Go to hobo camp and ask hoboes about the Muellers. Then she stood up and glanced at the big clock under the drugstore sign. "It's nearly three-thirty. We'd better not try to go to the hobo camp today, since I promised Mother I'd be home early. And we still have to talk to Roger's mother."

By the time the trio neared Roger's house, the sun was casting long shadows on the lawns and sidewalks of their neighborhood. They found Roger's mother outside, working in her flower bed.

"Those boys!" Roger's mother said when they told her their suspicions about Roger and Butch. "Sometimes I don't know what I'm going to do with Roger. As for Butch, I can't say it would surprise me if he took your dog home to keep for his own pet. Butch's father, Mr. Johnson, is a wealthy man, but he's always working. He pays so little attention to his son. And Butch's mother is dead, you know."

"No, ma'am," said Kit. "I didn't know. I . . . don't really know Butch." *No matter how lonely Butch was, he didn't have the right to take Grace,* she thought.

A PECULIAR FAMILY

Roger's mother sighed. "It's sad. Mr. Johnson is away so often on business trips. Butch stays alone in their big fancy house with only the housekeeper and handyman to keep an eye on him. They're a married couple who've worked for Mr. Johnson for years. It's usually one of them who drives Butch over here in that swanky Cadillac, not his father. But I'll try to get in touch with them and find out if Butch has Grace."

Impatience and frustration pinched at Kit as she and Stirling parted from Ruthie and headed for their own street. Every time it seemed that she was close to getting answers about Grace, more questions popped up—and more waiting.

At home, Kit helped Mother prepare the meal. Stirling went upstairs to take a bath because he and his mother had been invited to visit friends that evening after dinner. Kit realized that everyone would be going out for the evening, except her—and Miss McLenny.

After everyone ate, Miss McLenny went up to her room without a word. Kit was glad. The last thing she wanted to do was spend time alone with their grumpy new boarder.

When Kit had finished the dishes, she sat at the table to write in her notebook. On the Butch page, Kit made another entry in a separate column. She wrote Butch lonely (?) and under it:

Father out of town a lot. Butch stays alone in big house with housekeeper and handyman. They drive him around in a Cadillac.

She drew an arrow from kept Grace as his own to the new column to show that the two ideas were connected.

Kit finished writing and put down her pen. Everything was quiet in the house. The only sounds were the *tick-tick* of the kitchen clock and, through the open window, the chirping of crickets outside and the barking of a far-away dog.

Kit's throat felt tight. *Oh, Grace,* she thought, *where are you?*

A PECULIAR FAMILY

In Butch's big lonely house? With a poor hobo family? Or was she somewhere else entirely, somewhere Kit couldn't even guess? Kit swallowed painfully. "Wherever you are, Gracie," she whispered, "I'll find you."

Then she slammed her notebook shut, slipped it under her arm, and went upstairs to her room.

6
STRANGE HAPPENINGS ON RIVERVIEW LANE

In the morning, Kit, Stirling, and Ruthie headed for the hobo jungle. The day was another scorcher. The streets baked in the sun, and the air felt so steamy that it reminded Kit of the laundry where Dad used to take his shirts to be cleaned. At the hobo jungle, the humid air from the river made it seem even steamier.

Kit scanned the clearing. On a rope stretched between trees, heavily patched clothes were drying. Nearby, a woman was washing clothes in a big iron pot, and another was washing dishes. Throughout the camp, groups of hoboes were talking, eating, or sleeping on the ground. Barefoot, half-dressed children ran everywhere. Kit studied the camp, but she didn't see anyone who met the Muellers' description.

STRANGE HAPPENINGS

Heads turned to stare at Kit and her friends as they came into the clearing. No one spoke to them, or even smiled. Most of the hoboes went on with what they were doing as if Kit, Stirling, and Ruthie weren't even there.

Kit felt awkward. She wondered if it had been a mistake to come. Will had told her that hoboes were distrustful of strangers coming into their jungle. Would anyone here be willing to talk to them about the Muellers?

Then one group of hoboes caught Kit's attention. Two men and a woman were sitting together on the ground, listening to another man play a guitar and sing. Kit recognized the song, "Yellow Rose of Texas." Will had taught it to her. He'd said they sang it in Texas, where he was from.

Maybe this hobo is from Texas, too, Kit thought, *and maybe I can use the song to make friends with him.*

Kit gathered her courage, walked up to the man, and joined him in singing the chorus. The man grinned and strummed harder. He sang faster, and Kit did, too. The other men and the woman started clapping, and so did Ruthie and Stirling. Other hoboes gathered around to watch and listen. A few joined in.

When the song was over, everyone laughed and clapped. After that, the hoboes couldn't have been friendlier. They introduced themselves, using their hobo nicknames. The man who had sung with Kit was called "Guitar Tex," because he was from Texas. His friends' nicknames were Pig Train, Gats, and Deep South Sallie. Kit, Stirling, and Ruthie introduced themselves and told the hoboes why they were looking for the Muellers. Kit asked if the Muellers were still living at the hobo jungle.

"Oh, you mean Sunny and his folks," said Sallie in her southern drawl. She explained that Sunny got his nickname from his light blond hair. "Sorry, toots. They're gone."

"Do you know where they went?" Kit asked.

"From what I heard," said Sallie, "the mister got himself a right smart high-paying job. Moved the family somewhere called Riverside

Lane—no, that's not right. River*view*, it was.
Riverview Lane. Got himself a real house for
that wife of his to have her baby in."

"Yep, that's right," said Pig Train. "That's
what I heard." Guitar Tex said he'd heard the
same thing.

Gats leaned back against a stone and hooked
his fingers through the faded suspenders that
held up his too-short pants. "Reckon you'uns
don't know the whole story, though."

Sallie snorted. "And I suppose you *do*."

"As a matter of fact, I do," said Gats in a
self-important tone. Kit, Stirling, and Ruthie
turned interested eyes toward Gats.

"Then quit your crowing and spill the
beans," said Guitar Tex.

Gats looked offended, but he proceeded to
tell them what he knew. A man in a fancy suit,
Gats reported, had come to the hobo camp about
a week ago looking to hire one of the hoboes
for a job. Gats had wanted the job himself, but
the man had said that he wanted to help out a
man with a family to support. Gats had told him

about Sunny's father, whom Gats called German Jim, and the man had hired Mr. Mueller on the spot.

Kit thanked Gats for filling them in. Then she asked if they'd ever seen Sunny or his family in the hobo jungle with a basset hound.

"Lord-a-mercy, no!" said Sallie. "That poor man was desperate to find a way to feed his own family. Getting a dog would've been the last thing on his mind."

After the kids left the jungle, they sat on a bus-stop bench so that Kit could write in her notebook. On the page labeled The Muellers, next to Where do we find them?, she wrote: Riverview Lane. Underneath she wrote: Mueller boy has light blond hair. Hoboes call him "Sunny." Hoboes call Mr. Mueller "German Jim." She also put a note on the page that said: Hoboes say man in a fancy suit gave Mr. Mueller a job. Pays well.

"Now," she said, "all we have to do is find Riverview Lane."

"How do we do that?" wondered Ruthie. "I've never heard of that street."

"Simple," said Stirling. "We ask directions."

At a newsstand on the corner, they asked the man behind the counter how to get to Riverview Lane. He raised his eyebrows. "Are you sure you want to go there? It ain't the best neighborhood."

Kit assured him that they did, and the man told them how to find the street. Once they were on their way, Ruthie said, "How bad can the street be, with such a pretty name?"

They soon found out. They had only a few blocks to walk, but the closer they got, the more rundown and tough-looking the neighborhood became. When at last they turned onto Riverview Lane, they saw a row of small, dingy houses set on a steep hill, with privies behind. Trash from overflowing garbage cans littered the yards. Railroad tracks ran parallel to the street. Beyond the tracks was a cluster of trees, and behind the trees, the river.

Kit, Ruthie, and Stirling stood across the street and stared up at the houses. They looked as if they had once been painted white, but now the paint was gray and peeling. The front porches sagged like tired old men, and the steep wooden stairs that climbed the embankment from the street were missing steps. The tiny yards were little more than packed red earth and weeds.

In front of one house, two barefoot boys played marbles in the dirt. At another house, a smudge-faced toddler, clad only in a diaper, sat on the porch scraping food out of a bowl with her fingers as flies buzzed around her head and settled on the bowl. From an open window came angry voices: a man and a woman arguing.

In a yard scattered with dog droppings, a bony dog was chained to a post. The chain was so short, the dog could scarcely move, and the pitiful thing lay panting in the broiling sun. The dog was some kind of hound. *Probably a beagle*, Kit thought. Its long ears and brown, black, and white coloring reminded Kit of Grace, and Kit's heart did a flip-flop.

Is Grace inside one of these sad-looking houses? Kit wondered. *If she is, which one? Which of these houses is the Muellers'?*

STRANGE HAPPENINGS

Kit's thoughts were cut short when a fat, bald man came out of the house where the beagle was chained. The man lumbered down the porch steps, yelled at the dog in a mean voice, and walked to an old, beat-up Model T car parked in the yard. He cranked the car, and when it coughed to life, he got in and drove down the embankment and onto the street.

As the car *put-putted* toward Kit and her friends, the man stared so hard at them, it gave Kit the shivers.

"I hope *that's* not Mr. Mueller," Ruthie said.

Stirling shook his head. "I don't think so. He yelled at the dog in English, not German."

"Then that's one house we know *isn't* the Muellers'," said Kit. "Let's hurry and find out which one *is*."

"Yeah," Ruthie agreed, "before that man comes back."

The trio decided that the search would go faster if they split up. Since there were ten other houses on the street, each of them would ask about Grace at three of the houses. They would meet and go to the last house together.

At the first house Kit tried, no one answered her knock. She peered inside through a dirty window; no one seemed to be home. And there was no sign of a dog, not even in the backyard. Then in the backyard of the house next door, something caught Kit's eye: diapers hung out on a droopy clothesline. Those people had a baby. Maybe that was the Muellers' house!

Kit hurried around to the front and up onto the rickety porch. Through an open window, she heard a baby fussing and someone coughing. *Mrs. Mueller, perhaps?* The pet-store owner and the soup-kitchen director had both said that Mrs. Mueller was ill.

Kit raised her hand to the door and knocked. She listened, hoping to hear a dog barking. But the only thing she heard was footsteps—someone coming to answer the door.

Then the door opened, and Kit was looking into the face of a boy about her age—a boy with hair so blond, it was almost the color of corn silk. *Sunny.*

STRANGE HAPPENINGS

For a moment Sunny did nothing but stare at Kit. She tried to look past him, into the house, hoping to catch a glimpse of a basset hound, but it was too dark inside to see anything. "Hello," Kit finally said.

"Hello," said Sunny, in a not-too-friendly tone.

He didn't say anything else, so Kit spoke up. "I've lost my basset hound, and I think your family might have gotten her by mistake. Your last name *is* Mueller, isn't it?"

Sunny drew in a sharp breath. *He's surprised,* Kit thought. *Is it because I know his name? Or does he know something about Grace?*

"Please," Kit begged, her voice catching. "If you've seen my dog, or know where she is, *please* help me. I have to get her back."

Sunny's cheeks flushed. Quickly he turned and shot a nervous glance behind him. Then he turned back to Kit and said, "Come inside."

For a moment Kit was afraid. What if Mr. Mueller was as mean as the man in the Model T? She had the urge to run away, but she fought it.

Instead, she stepped over the threshold, into the house. Sunny closed the door behind her with a *thud*.

The room in which Kit stood was small and dim, and completely bare of furniture. A stale, unpleasant odor hung in the air. Cooked cabbage, Kit thought, and dirty diapers.

"Wait here," Sunny said. He turned and disappeared down a dark hallway. Kit heard the *click* of a door opening, and muffled voices. Then she heard footsteps, heavier than the boy's, coming toward her down the hall. Again she was afraid. *Why did I come inside alone?* she thought. *Why didn't I go back for Stirling and Ruthie?*

A man emerged from the dark hallway. He was so thin that his cheekbones jutted out, and the sharp features of his face gave him a sinister look. But then the man smiled, and Kit relaxed a little. "How can I help you, *Fräulein?*" he asked in a heavy German accent.

"I . . . um . . . think your son might have found my dog, Grace." Kit's voice shook with nervousness. She took a breath to steady it and went on. "Someone saw him a few days ago at the park with a basset hound that looked like Grace. And—" She started to add, *And the pet-store owner saw **you** later with the same dog.*

But the man was already shaking his head. "You are mistaken. My son is *allergisch* ... how you say in English? Allergic? Dogs are not good for my son. He cannot be near dogs. Give him red bumps all over. Make him very sick. No dog for us. Understand?"

Kit felt her jaw drop open. This was the last answer she had expected: that the Muellers not only didn't have Grace, or a basset hound that *looked* like Grace, but they'd never had *any* dog.

The man was going on. "Now, *Fräulein*, I am sorry, but I must ask you to leave. We are expecting a guest." He opened the front door and gestured her toward it. His smile was gone, and his eyes were hard and unfriendly.

"S-sorry to bother you," she stammered. She turned and hurried out the door and down the porch steps, two at a time. She felt eyes boring into her back and whirled around just in time to see a face disappear from the Muellers' window. A chill rippled down her spine. Was Mr. Mueller watching her? Or was it Sunny?

Kit had no desire to find out. All she wanted to do was get away from the Muellers, from their rundown house, from the whole grim neighborhood. Suddenly it seemed that the worst thing in the world would be to find Grace *anywhere* on Riverview Lane.

7
THE CADILLAC MAN

Kit flew down the rickety steps of the embankment to the street. Then she saw Ruthie and Stirling hurrying toward her. Kit waited for them, trying to catch her breath. "What's wrong, Kit?" said Ruthie when they had caught up with her.

"Yeah, what happened at that house?" Stirling asked.

Kit told them about her strange visit at the Muellers'. "Maybe I imagined the face at the window, but there was something about Mr. Mueller that gave me the most uneasy feeling..."

"Were you *afraid* of him?" asked Ruthie.

"Not exactly," said Kit. "Not at first, anyway." She gave a frustrated sigh. "Oh, I can't explain it."

"*I* can explain it," said Stirling. "That man was *lying* to you, and you must have sensed it. The family at the pet store had to be the Muellers, so they *did* have a dog last Saturday. It might not have been Grace, but it was definitely a dog."

"Why would Mr. Mueller lie about something as innocent as having a dog?" Ruthie said.

"Maybe it *wasn't* so innocent," Kit interrupted. Ruthie's eyes widened.

"Something about the Muellers is fishy," said Kit. "They've got *something* to hide, and it has to do with that basset hound they had at the pet store."

"Do you think that dog was Grace?" Ruthie asked.

Kit looked up at the Muellers' house. "I don't know—maybe. But I'm sure of one thing. Grace isn't there now. Even if they'd had her hidden somewhere, she would've barked when she heard my voice." Kit swallowed hard. "So I guess we might as well go home."

Kit was too discouraged to talk as they began walking up Riverview Lane. They had almost made it to the street's end when a big, light-colored car with a hood ornament careened around the corner onto Riverview and sped past them.

The friends turned and looked at the car. "Isn't that a Cadillac?" asked Kit.

"Sure is," Stirling replied.

"Why would someone rich enough to own a Cadillac come to this neighborhood?" Ruthie asked.

As they watched, the Cadillac pulled up in front of the Muellers' house and stopped. A man in a blue business suit and hat got out of the car and began to climb the steps up the embankment.

Halfway up the stairs, a gusty breeze blew off the man's hat, and he stooped to pick it up. As he placed it back on his head, Kit felt a twinge in the back of her mind. Before she could think more about it, the man had reached the Muellers' porch and gone up to the door. He lifted his hand to knock, but before he could do so, the door opened, and the man disappeared inside.

"Jeepers," said Ruthie, "they were sure expecting *him*."

"Yeah," Kit agreed, "and for some reason they wanted to make sure *I* wasn't there when he arrived."

"Maybe that's why one of the Muellers was watching you out the window, Kit," said Ruthie. "To make sure you were gone before the Cadillac man arrived."

"'The Cadillac man'," Kit said. "It fits him. He's a bit mysterious."

"How so?" asked Stirling.

"His car, for one thing." Kit glanced in that direction. "A Cadillac with whitewall tires and a hood ornament. Awful fancy car for a place like this."

Stirling frowned. "It looks a lot like the Cadillac that came through *our* neighborhood the other day."

"Yes!" Kit remembered the twinge she'd felt when the Cadillac man's hat blew off his head. She told Ruthie and Stirling. "It was because his hat was a *fedora*. And the driver of the Cadillac in our neighborhood was wearing a fedora, too."

"Lots of men wear fedoras, Kit," said Ruthie. "My father wears one every day to work."

"Lots of people drive Cadillacs, too," commented Stirling. "Like Butch's father."

"Hey!" said Ruthie. "Maybe that Cadillac is *his*."

Stirling looked at her a little doubtfully. "I guess it's *possible*."

Ruthie grimaced. "Is that too far-fetched?"

"No idea is too far-fetched if it helps us find Grace," said Kit. "We think Butch had something to do with Grace's disappearance. And we know his father has a Cadillac. The Muellers have—or had—a mystery dog, a basset hound. And a Cadillac shows up here. *I* think we should check it out."

"How?" asked Stirling.

"We could wait until the Cadillac man leaves," suggested Ruthie, "and follow him. See where he goes."

"On foot?" said Stirling. "And him in a car? There's no way we could keep up with him.

He'd get away from us in no time."

"Maybe we wouldn't have to *follow* him to find out more about him," Kit said. "Stirling, do you remember that Dick Tracy comic we were reading the other day?" Dick Tracy was a police detective in a comic strip in the newspaper.

"Which one?" Stirling asked. "We read Dick Tracy *every* day."

"The one where Dick foiled bank robbers by tracing the license plate number on their getaway car."

"Oh, yeah," said Stirling.

"We could do the same thing," Kit said. "We could find out who the Cadillac man is by tracing the license plate number on *his* car. It'd give us his name at least, and then we could go from there."

Stirling wrinkled his forehead. "One problem with that, Kit. Only the police can trace license plates. Since we don't have proof that a crime's been committed, we can't really go to the police and ask them to trace the plate number."

"*Somebody* stole Grace—" Kit began.

"But we can't *prove* anything," said Stirling. "The police aren't going to listen to us without some evidence."

"*I* know a policeman who'd listen to us," said Ruthie. "Sergeant Paul. If he isn't out on patrol, I know he'll at least take the time to hear us out. And the station where he works is at the corner of Grant and Elm, which is on our way home."

Kit pulled the notebook out of her pocket and jotted down the license number. "We can fill Sergeant Paul in on everything else we've learned, too. But there's more I need to write down first."

They walked over to the next street and sat down on the curb. Kit started a new page in her notebook. She wrote **Strange Happenings on Riverview Lane** at the top. Below the title, she made a list that said:

- Sunny's strange behavior: stared at me, seemed nervous. (Does he know something about Grace?)

- Mr. Mueller lied about having a dog.
- Somebody was watching me from the window.
- Light-colored Cadillac with whitewall tires and hood ornament pulls up to Muellers' house (similar to Cadillac in our neighborhood? Possibly Butch's father's car?).
- Someone rich enough to own a Cadillac—hereafter called Cadillac man—comes to visit hobo family (the Muellers).
- Cadillac man wears a fedora. Driver of Cadillac in our neighborhood also wore fedora.

At the bottom of the page, she wrote:

Questions: Where is the dog the Muellers had at the pet store? Who does the Cadillac on Riverview Lane belong to? Who was driving the Cadillac in our neighborhood?

Then she turned to the **Our Investigation** page and wrote: Ask Sergeant Paul if he can trace license number of Cadillac.

THE CADILLAC MAN

After Kit finished writing, they headed
to Police Precinct No. 5, where Sergeant Paul
worked. The station was a redbrick and stone
building that took up most of the city block.
Inside, they found Sergeant Paul in his office.
Ruthie asked if he had time to talk to them.

"For my future niece and her friends, I'll
make time," he said.

Kit showed Sergeant Paul her notebook, and
the friends explained how their clues seemed
to lead in two different directions. "Some of the
clues lead to a rich boy—Butch," said Kit.

"But the other clues lead to a boy who hardly
has anything," said Ruthie.

Kit also told Sergeant Paul about the similar Cadillacs they'd seen in their neighborhood
and at the Muellers', and explained that Butch's
father also had a Cadillac.

"We want to know who the Cadillac we
saw on Riverview Lane belongs to," said Kit,
"whether it belongs to Butch's father or someone
else. Ruthie said you might be able to trace the
license plate number."

Sergeant Paul tapped his pencil on his desk. "Well," he said, "it would be a bit irregular, but let me see what I can do." Then he said that his shift was over and he was getting ready to leave. "Can I give you kids a lift home?" he offered. "I'm driving the squad car."

They eagerly accepted. Twenty minutes later, Sergeant Paul was dropping them off in front of Ruthie's house. Aunt Nancy came out when she saw the squad car, and Paul and the kids filled her in. She invited Paul to come inside, but he said he needed to get home, that he'd been out all night on police business and hadn't slept in twenty-four hours.

"Are you still short on staff?" Aunt Nancy asked. She looked concerned.

He nodded and blew out a tired sigh. "The police department is short of money, like everyone else. We can't hire enough officers to handle all we have to do, so we work harder to make up for it."

"I know you've been busy," said Nancy. "But I wondered if you'd heard anything more about these show-dog thefts you mentioned the other day. I saw in the paper this morning that one was stolen from *our* neighborhood yesterday."

Kit's attention snapped to Nancy and Paul's conversation.

"I don't know much," said Sergeant Paul. "I'm not working on that case myself, but a buddy of mine is. He says the thief seems to know what he's doing, somehow tracking down the most valuable show dogs in the city to steal.

"The investigation keeps getting stalled because more serious cases come up. With the police force stretched so thin, we don't have the manpower to make much progress on the dog thefts. Listen, I've got to go. Got to get some sleep."

"Poor dear," said Nancy, touching his shoulder. "You'll let us know if you find out anything about the license plate? It means so much to the kids."

"Yes, I know it does," said Sergeant Paul, glancing at Kit and her friends. "I'll do my best."

8
KIT'S HUNCH

Kit spent the next morning helping Mother peel and cook tomatoes for Mother's special spaghetti sauce. Then Mother said Kit and Stirling could go to Ruthie's. Kit's Missing Dog column had been in yesterday's newspaper, and Kit was eager to call Gibb's office to see if there had been any responses.

Ruthie looked up the number for the *Register* in the phone book, and Kit called Gibb's secretary, Miss Preston.

"Why, yes," Miss Preston said. "We've had several calls about your dog. Hold on, and I'll get the information for you." Kit waited a few moments. She heard papers shuffling in the background. Then Miss Preston came back on the line.

Kit's Hunch

"Here we are," Miss Preston said. She read off a dozen names of people who had responded, along with their addresses and phone numbers, and Kit wrote them down in her notebook. Miss Preston promised to call Ruthie's house if any more responses came in.

Kit made the phone calls, since Grace belonged to her. Each time Kit got her hopes up, but each time she was disappointed. All she had to do was hear the people's descriptions of the dogs they'd found to know they weren't Grace.

That evening Aunt Nancy took Kit, Ruthie, and Stirling to visit a couple of people who'd responded to the story but didn't have phones. They'd called from neighbors' houses or nearby stores. At one address no one was home. The other person had found a basset hound that seemed to have mismatched parts. Its ears were too short, its legs too long, and its head too small. It was the homeliest basset hound Kit had ever seen. *Definitely* not Grace.

On the drive home, Kit asked Aunt Nancy if she'd heard anything from Sergeant Paul about the license plate. "Not yet," Aunt Nancy replied. "I'm sure he'll get back to us as soon as he can."

The next morning Kit was in the middle of doing her chores when Ruthie came over. Stirling wasn't home; he'd gotten a job for the week doing work around the house and yard for his mother's boss. Kit was by herself in the upstairs hall putting clean sheets away in the linen closet when she heard her mother greet Ruthie at the front door. A minute later, Ruthie came running up the stairs.

"Guess what?" Ruthie said, her cheeks flushed with excitement. "Sergeant Paul called Aunt Nancy last night about the Cadillac's license plate."

Kit, her heartbeat quickening, turned to Ruthie. "Who does the Cadillac belong to? Butch's father?"

"Nope," said Ruthie. "The owner's not a

person at all. It's a kennel out in the country. Shy-Anne Kennel. Aunt Nancy called the kennel owner this morning. Guess what kind of dogs they raise?"

"Just tell me," Kit said eagerly.

Ruthie stepped closer. "They raise *basset hounds*, Kit, and beagles, too. Champion hounds, the man said. Show dogs."

"Basset hounds?" Kit sat down hard in a chair near the linen closet, still holding a folded sheet. "*That* can't be a coincidence. The same kind of dog the Muellers just happened to have with them at the pet store. And those show dogs that Sergeant Paul mentioned—weren't they basset hounds, too?"

"Hey, you're right," said Ruthie. "I forgot about the stolen basset hounds. I was thinking of the Muellers' mystery dog, and of Grace—"

"I'm thinking of Grace, too," said Kit. "And Mr. Mueller's fishy behavior, and the two Cadillacs, and the two fedoras, and the way Sunny stared at me when I asked if he'd found my basset hound." She stood up, put the sheet down on the chair, and paced to the window. She stared out over the landscape of peak-roofed houses, shaggy treetops, and winding streets. "And then there are the stolen show dogs—at least some of those were basset hounds. And now a *kennel* that raises basset hounds. Basset hounds and Cadillacs and fedoras..."

Kit turned to face Ruthie. "It's all been rattling around in my brain—all the clues and everything I've written in my notebook. I can't stop thinking about it, and the harder I think, the more tangled up it all gets." Kit put her hands to her head for a moment and then, with a heavy sigh, dropped them. "But I have a feeling that somewhere in the tangle, there's that one clue that will set us on the right track to finding Grace."

Ruthie's eyes shone. "I know what you mean, Kit. All along we've been following these two different trails of clues, as if they *both* could lead us to Grace. But both trails can't do that. *One* of them has to be the *wrong* trail. We have to figure out which is the *right* one."

"I'm beginning to think the wrong trail is the Muellers," said Kit.

"But the basset hound they had at the pet store—"

"Maybe it was one of the *stolen* basset hounds," suggested Kit.

Ruthie blinked. "Huh?"

"Think about it, Ruthie. The man at the pet store couldn't understand how the Muellers could have such a fine-looking dog. A show dog would be a very fine-looking dog, wouldn't it?"

"Of course," said Ruthie.

"Then there's Mr. Mueller's job," Kit went on. "Gats said that a man in a fancy suit had offered Mr. Mueller a job. Fancy suits cost a lot of money, and so do Cadillacs. Maybe the man who gave Mr. Mueller a job was the Cadillac man—and maybe the job was *stealing dogs*. Maybe the Cadillac man and the Muellers are the *dog thieves*."

Understanding showed on Ruthie's face. "Someone from a kennel *would* know what he was doing when it came to stealing champion dogs. *And* it would explain why Mr. Mueller didn't tell the soup-kitchen workers that he'd gotten a job. He couldn't very well tell them he was doing something *illegal*."

Kit nodded. "And it explains why Mr. Mueller got upset when I mentioned that someone had seen his son at the park with a basset hound— a basset hound that I thought was Grace. *Mr. Mueller* didn't know that the show dog his son stole wasn't the same dog I was looking for."

"Maybe we've stumbled upon something that'll help the police solve the dog-theft case," said Ruthie.

"Maybe," said Kit. She felt torn. It was exciting to think they might have discovered an important clue that would help the police. But what about *Grace?*

Basset hounds and Cadillacs... Kit's own words echoed in her head. It was hard to believe that all these similarities were just coincidences. Deep inside, Kit felt as if the show-dog thefts must be connected to Grace's disappearance, but she couldn't find the link. *Grace* wasn't a show dog. Still, Kit felt sure she was missing something. What was it?

"We've got to figure this out," said Kit. "If you'll help me put away this laundry, we can go somewhere and think it through."

With both girls working, they were soon finished with the laundry. On the back porch, a breeze came through the screen, and the girls settled in porch chairs with Kit's notebook. Kit started a new page called **Show-Dog Thefts** and wrote down everything they had thought of. Under the title, she wrote Cadillac at the Muellers' registered to Shy-Anne Kennel. Could someone from the kennel be the show-dog thief?

Beneath it she wrote another question: Could the Cadillac man and the Muellers be the thieves?

Suddenly Kit looked up. A thought had jolted her. "Ruthie! Come on. I have an idea. Let's go to the library."

"Sure," Ruthie said. "But why?"

"I want to check something out," said Kit, "but not a book."

"What, then?"

"Oh," Kit said mysteriously, "nothing much. Just a hunch I have."

Kit wouldn't tell Ruthie anything about her hunch until they were at the library. Then Kit would only say that she wanted to look up newspaper reports about the dog thefts. Since the girls didn't know exactly when the thefts had occurred, they worked backward. Starting with the newspaper from that morning—Thursday—they began scouring the local news sections of the *Register*, looking for any mention of the thefts.

In Sunday morning's newspaper they saw the article Sergeant Paul had mentioned about the first two show dogs that had been stolen. Every day since Sunday, articles about the thefts had been in the paper. Two more basset hounds had disappeared, including the show dog stolen from their own neighborhood on Monday. It was the most recent theft.

As soon as Kit started reading the article about that theft, she felt her heart bounce. The stolen dog was Mr. Panetta's basset hound,

Roland! Kit read the article twice, then pushed the newspaper toward Ruthie. "Look! Read this," she said.

As Ruthie read, her mouth fell open in disbelief. She looked up at Kit. "Mr. Panetta from the park! His basset hound was stolen right out of his backyard."

"Almost exactly the way Grace was stolen," said Kit. "I think we ought to go visit Mr. Panetta and find out more about Roland's theft."

"I do, too," said Ruthie.

"We'll go after dinner tonight," said Kit, "when Mr. Panetta has had time to get home from work. For now, let's read more about the thefts. When we're finished, I'll tell you about my hunch."

The girls studied the articles, and Kit took notes. Finally they pieced together what they thought had happened in all the dog thefts, and how the thefts compared to Grace's disappearance. Kit jotted down everything in her notebook. She titled the page Missing Dogs and made a list of the facts.

MISSING GRACE

What happened: Show dogs stolen—four basset hounds, three males and one female. Ordinary dogs stolen—One basset hound (Grace), female.

When, where, how it happened: Separate times and places within the last week.

- One dog stolen when left alone in a parked car.
- One dog stolen from a house while owner was at work (thief broke a window to get inside).
- One dog disappeared when owner tied him up outside a diner and went in to buy a cup of coffee. (Owner: "I was inside for only five minutes.")
- One dog disappeared from a backyard (Mr. Panetta's dog, Roland).
- One dog disappeared from our back porch (Grace).

Similarities: All basset hounds. Every dog except Grace was a champion show dog worth hundreds of dollars. Two dogs (Grace and Roland) disappeared from the same neighborhood under similar circumstances within a few days of each other.

At the bottom of the page Kit wrote in large letters:

Were Grace and Roland taken by the same person?
Did Cadillac man and Muellers take Grace?

Ruthie looked surprised. "You think the *dog thieves* might have taken Grace? But Mrs. Cox saw *Butch* with Grace. And so did the lady at the park."

"They saw Grace with a boy who had blond hair," said Kit. "Sunny Mueller has blond hair, too."

"Yes, but—" Ruthie began.

Kit leaned toward Ruthie. "The Muellers had a fine-looking basset hound with them at the pet store. Three days later, when we visited Riverview Lane, that dog had mysteriously disappeared. Then a Cadillac shows up at the Muellers'—a Cadillac that looks like the one we saw in *our* neighborhood, *right before Grace disappeared.*"

Ruthie's cheeks flushed with excitement. "The Cadillac in our neighborhood could be the same one we saw at the Muellers'!"

"Exactly." Kit leaned closer to Ruthie. "And there were three people in that Cadillac: the driver with a fedora, and a man and a boy."

"The Cadillac man, Mr. Mueller, and Sunny!" said Ruthie.

"It fits all our clues," said Kit.

"The only thing that *doesn't* fit is *why*," said Ruthie. "If the Muellers *are* the dog thieves, why would they want to steal *Grace?* She's not an expensive show dog."

"That's what I can't figure out," said Kit. "It's the part of my hunch that doesn't make sense. I thought the Cadillac might be the thread that tied together the Muellers, the dog thefts, and Grace. I was hoping to find some mention of the Cadillac in the newspaper articles about the thefts."

"But we didn't find anything."

"It could be that the Cadillac was there at the scene of some of the dog thefts, but no one knew to look for it," said Kit. "We need to ask Mr. Panetta about a Cadillac when we go see him this evening."

"And maybe we can find out more about the Cadillac when we go to Shy-Anne Kennel," said Ruthie. "I forgot to tell you—Aunt Nancy promised to take us tomorrow."

"Oh, good," said Kit. She wrote both their ideas in her notebook under **Our Investigation.**

After dinner Kit and Ruthie walked over to Hedgerow Place. They had looked up Mr. Panetta's address in the phone book. Mr. Panetta was mowing grass in his front yard.

When he saw them, he stopped pushing the lawn mower. "Hello," he said, mopping his forehead with a handkerchief. "Aren't you the young ladies from the park with the lost basset hound?"

"Yes," said Kit. She introduced herself and Ruthie. "Only my dog, Grace, wasn't exactly lost. Someone took her."

"Right off Kit's back porch," said Ruthie.

Mr. Panetta's eyes narrowed. *"Really."*

"We read in the paper about *Roland* being stolen," said Ruthie.

"Out of *your* backyard," said Kit.

"It was quite a shock," said Mr. Panetta sadly. "And if you read about Roland, you probably know that a number of valuable show dogs have been stolen recently. Was your basset a show dog?"

Kit shook her head. "But the way Grace disappeared seems awfully similar to the way Roland disappeared."

"That's why we came over to talk to you," said Ruthie. "We were hoping you could tell us something that might help us find Grace."

"I don't know about that," said Mr. Panetta, "but I'll certainly tell you anything you want to know about Roland."

"When we saw you at the park," Kit said,

"we had no idea that Roland was a show dog."

"He looked like an ordinary basset hound to us," said Ruthie.

Mr. Panetta chuckled. "That's not surprising. Only someone who truly knows the breed would recognize the difference between a champion show dog like Roland and a pet basset hound like your Grace."

"Golly," said Ruthie. "Roland is a *champion?*"

Mr. Panetta smiled. "Yes, Roland is a champion and bred from champions. His mother won top honors at Westminster."

"Westminster?" asked Kit.

"Westminster is the most prestigious dog show in the country," Mr. Panetta replied. "I'd hoped Roland might someday compete there and do as well as his mother. His pedigree was so promising . . ."

"What's a pedigree?" asked Ruthie.

"It's a record of a dog's parents and grandparents and so on," Mr. Panetta explained. "A pedigree can be traced back many generations. I paid hundreds of dollars for Roland based on his pedigree alone."

"A dog is worth *that* much money because of who its parents are?" said Ruthie.

"Yes, indeed," Mr. Panetta replied. "But the more shows a dog like Roland wins, the more valuable he becomes. A dog that has the potential to win a national dog-show title like Westminster could eventually be worth thousands of dollars. I've tried to enter Roland in every dog show I can. He was the favorite to win the Labor Day Dog Show here in Cincinnati next weekend."

Mr. Panetta glanced away for a moment. "Please excuse me," he said in a thick voice. "I'm still upset over Roland's theft."

"I know how you feel!" said Kit.

Mr. Panetta gave Kit a sad smile and then went on. "Pedigrees are very important. When you're buying a puppy that's going to be a show dog, you want to buy from the most reputable dog breeder you can find. Like Shy-Anne Kennel, where Roland was born. Shy-Anne is one of the most notable breeders of basset hounds in the country, and Roland's mother was the kennel's winning-est dog ever."

"Shy-Anne Kennel!" the girls exclaimed at the same time.

Mr. Panetta looked surprised. "You know the kennel?"

Kit and Ruthie glanced at each other. "We've . . . heard of it," Ruthie stammered.

There was a moment of silence. Then Kit said, "Mr. Panetta, we were wondering something. Did you happen to see a Cadillac in your neighborhood the day Roland was stolen?"

Mr. Panetta scratched his head as he thought, and then he looked at the girls with a surprised expression. "Come to think of it, there was a Cadillac parked across the street when I got home from walking Roland at the park on Monday. I wondered if the neighbors had gotten a new car. Why?"

"It's probably nothing," said Kit. She didn't want to tell Mr. Panetta her suspicions about the Cadillac from Shy-Anne Kennel, since he thought so highly of the place.

"What did you do with Roland," asked Ruthie, "after you got home?"

"I put him inside the fence in the backyard because my wife and I were going shopping later. He disappeared while we were out."

"One more question," said Kit. "When you got home from shopping, did you notice whether the Cadillac was still parked across the street?"

Mr. Panetta considered a moment. "You know, I don't believe it was. I think the Cadillac was gone."

Just then Mr. Panetta's wife opened the door and came out on the porch. "Tony! Dinner's ready," she called. "Oh, hello," she said to the girls.

Mr. Panetta introduced the girls to his wife and told her that Kit's basset hound had also been stolen. "Dear me," said Mrs. Panetta. "It's awful, isn't it? For someone to go around stealing people's beloved dogs?"

The girls said they certainly agreed, and Mr. and Mrs. Panetta went in to dinner.

Before Kit and Ruthie left, they sat on the

curb while Kit wrote more in her notebook. She started a new page called **Similarities between Grace's and Roland's Disappearance**. Then she made a list:

• Grace and Roland disappeared from owner's property within days of each other. (Grace from back porch, Roland from backyard.)
• Cadillac nearby when Roland was taken. Cadillac drove by the day before Grace was taken.

Below the list she jotted:

Note: Roland was born at Shy-Anne Kennel. (Unknown where Grace was born.)
Cadillac registered to Shy-Anne Kennel.

In big letters she added: **Who is the Cadillac man??? Find out tomorrow at Shy-Anne Kennel!**

9
WINNING-EST DOG EVER

The next morning, Aunt Nancy, Kit, and Ruthie piled into Aunt Nancy's convertible and headed out of the city. Shy-Anne Kennel was located near a village called Scottsboro, about ten miles from Cincinnati. The owner of the kennel, a man named Mr. Watkins, had given Aunt Nancy directions over the phone.

On the drive there, Aunt Nancy confessed to the girls that she'd told Mr. Watkins she might be interested in buying a puppy. "It's the truth; I've been wanting a dog. Now is as good a time as any to start looking. And I had to give the man a reason for wanting to come out to the kennel. Play along, girls, if you will. And let's hope we find out something about that Cadillac while we're puppy shopping."

"And maybe about Grace, too?" said Kit.

"Yes," said Aunt Nancy. "Most of all let's hope we can find out something that will lead us to Grace."

After they passed through Scottsboro, it was another two miles to the kennel along an unpaved, twisting country lane, and then up a gravel driveway to a white house set in a cluster of trees. A short distance from the house was a long, low wooden building with connecting fenced-in dog runs and an ornate sign that read *Shy-Anne Kennel, Champion Basset Hounds and Beagles.*

Nervous tension pulled at Kit's chest. In a few minutes, she'd be face-to-face with Mr. Watkins, the Cadillac man. Aunt Nancy parked in front of the kennel. She and the girls got out of the car and went up to the kennel's front door. The door was locked. "That's funny," said Aunt Nancy. "Mr. Watkins *knew* we were coming."

"I'll tell you what else is funny," said Kit. "There're no dogs in the dog runs. And listen. No barking."

"Maybe the dogs are inside," Ruthie suggested.

Aunt Nancy shook her head. "In this heat, the windows would have to be open to give the dogs some air. Then you would hear barking."

"The windows are all closed," said Kit. Then she glanced at the long chain-link dog runs at the side of the building. The cement floors were spotless—not a stain, a single dog dropping, or even a wisp of fur in sight. "And the dog runs are way too clean," she added.

"Yeah," said Ruthie. "Doesn't look as if dogs have been kept here for a while."

Kit frowned. "Where's Mr. Watkins?" she asked Aunt Nancy. "Was he supposed to meet you here?"

"He didn't say," Aunt Nancy replied. "I just assumed he would keep puppies in the kennel. Let's go on up to the house. Maybe Mr. Watkins is waiting for us there."

"Would it be all right if we peeked inside the kennel first?" Kit asked.

Aunt Nancy glanced around, then nodded.

The three of them walked across the gravel in front of the building and peered in a window beside the front door. The room inside looked as if it had once been used as an office. Open filing cabinets stood against one wall, their drawers pulled out and empty. The rest of the room was bare. The walls were discolored in places where it looked as if pictures had once hung.

Then they looked in another window, toward the back of the building. They saw a huge kennel area, with dog pens on both sides and a walkway between. But every pen was empty and as spotless as the dog runs outside.

"Obviously this building isn't being used for a kennel any longer," said Aunt Nancy. "I don't understand it, if Mr. Watkins is still selling puppies."

The kennel's abandoned air made Kit feel even more nervous than she had felt before. "And what about the Cadillac?" she said. "We haven't seen that, either."

Ruthie pointed to a small building behind the kennel. "Hey, that looks like a garage. And the doors are open. Maybe the Cadillac's in there."

Kit started across the grass toward the garage, with Aunt Nancy and Ruthie at her heels. Peering into the shadowy interior, they saw a green Buick sedan, but no Cadillac.

"So where do you think the Cadillac is?" asked Kit.

"Who knows?" said Aunt Nancy. "This all seems a bit strange. If Mr. Watkins is up at the house, maybe we can ask some questions and find out. But remember, we're supposed to be puppy shopping. Our questions can't be too obvious."

They returned to the driveway and walked up to the house. Aunt Nancy rang the doorbell. A few moments passed. Then a grandfatherly man with a white mane of hair and a close-cropped white beard answered and introduced himself as Mr. Watkins, the kennel's owner.

Kit blinked. *This* couldn't be the Cadillac man. He'd been clean-shaven and *much* younger. Kit looked quizzically at Ruthie. Ruthie shook her head, looking as puzzled as Kit felt.

Winning-est Dog Ever

Aunt Nancy introduced them all, and
Mr. Watkins invited them inside. He showed
them into his living room and asked them to
be seated. "I like to chat awhile with prospective
buyers," he said. "I feel strongly about my puppies getting into the right homes."

Nancy asked him about the kennel's
deserted look. Mr. Watkins said he was closing
the business. "I'm retiring, after fifty years of
dog breeding. Everything but the building and
this last litter of puppies has already been sold."

"It must be sad to close your kennel, Mr.
Watkins," said Ruthie.

"In some ways it's a relief," Mr. Watkins
said quietly. "Ever since the Depression began,
we've struggled to stay in business. Little by little,
I had to sell most of my dogs, and I had to let my
employees go, one by one. The last few years, we
ran the kennel on a shoestring, just me, my wife,
and one loyal trainer. Then my wife got sick . . ."

He stopped for a moment and dabbed at
his eyes. "After she died, I didn't have the heart
to continue the business. So I decided to sell

everything and shut the kennel down."

"That must have been very difficult," said Aunt Nancy. "Selling everything after so many years—all your dogs, your equipment, your vehicles."

Vehicles, thought Kit. *Aunt Nancy is trying to find out whether he sold the Cadillac.*

"Yes," said Mr. Watkins with a sigh. "But it's done now. All but the building sold weeks ago."

That explains why the Cadillac wasn't in the garage, Kit thought. Whoever had bought it must be the Cadillac man! But who was the new owner? How could Kit get Mr. Watkins to say?

Before she could think of a way, Mr. Watkins had changed the subject. "I've bored you long enough with my troubles. Miss Smithens, you said you were interested in getting a basset hound puppy."

Aunt Nancy nodded. "My niece and her friend came along to help me make a choice. Kit here owns a fine basset hound herself." She paused and then added forcefully, "Kit's dog is *missing* at the moment."

Kit caught on. Aunt Nancy was trying to see how Mr. Watkins would react to a mention of Grace. Kit sat up straighter in her chair. "Yes, my basset hound, Grace, disappeared off our back porch. We think she was stolen."

"Of course," Aunt Nancy said hurriedly, "Grace wasn't a *show dog* like the other basset hounds that have disappeared. I imagine you've heard of those thefts, haven't you, Mr. Watkins?"

"Oh, yes!" said Mr. Watkins. "It's been quite distressing. Every one of the stolen bassets was an exceptionally fine show dog. In fact, they were all born right here at our kennel." Surprised glances shot between Kit, Aunt Nancy, and Ruthie. Before Kit could say anything, Mr. Watkins went on. "Over the years, Shy-Anne has produced some of the best basset hounds in the country, you know."

Mr. Watkins looked at Kit. "Have you reported your dog's theft to the police?" he asked. "If you haven't, you really should."

Kit was perplexed. Mr. Watkins certainly

didn't sound like a thief.

Then Mr. Watkins stood up. "I hope you're ready to see some fine puppies. This is the last litter for my top female basset, Walhampton Day-Dawn—Dawn for short. She's getting too old to breed.

"Dawn was once a national champion, as were many of her puppies. And Dawn herself was bred from champions. If you'll look there on the wall, you'll see her registration papers from the American Kennel Club—AKC for short. I keep Dawn's papers on display for potential puppy buyers to see." With a wave of his hand, Mr. Watkins beckoned them over.

Aunt Nancy, Kit, and Ruthie got up to look at the large framed document on the wall. "This is interesting," Aunt Nancy remarked.

"Golly," said Ruthie, "it's a long list of names."

"What does it all mean?" asked Kit.

"The papers list the owner's name and address and the dog's pedigree," Mr. Watkins explained. "Whenever someone buys a purebred dog, the new owner is supposed to register the dog in his own name with the AKC. That way the AKC can keep up with every dog's pedigree."

"Suppose I bought one of your puppies," Aunt Nancy said. "How would I go about getting the puppy registered?"

"We have blank registration forms here for each dog," he said. "When you buy your puppy, I give you the form for your dog, you fill it out with your name as the owner, and then you send it in to the AKC to make the registration—and the pedigree—official."

"All that trouble just to keep up with a dog's pedigree?" asked Ruthie.

Mr. Watkins laughed. "It's the pedigree that makes a dog valuable. And you can't enter a dog in shows unless it has papers. So the trouble is well worth it."

Kit studied Dawn's pedigree while Mr. Watkins talked about all the dog-show awards Dawn's parents and grandparents had won. "But Dawn's awards have surpassed them all," he added, beaming with pride. "In fact, Dawn has been Shy-Anne Kennel's winning-est dog ever."

Kit looked up sharply. *Winning-est dog ever—that's what Mr. Panetta said about Roland's mother,* she thought. Roland must have been one of Dawn's puppies!

Kit asked Mr. Watkins if he remembered Mr. Panetta and Roland and whether he knew that Roland had been stolen.

"Yes, on both counts," said Mr. Watkins. "Mr. Panetta called to tell me about Roland's theft the day after it happened."

"Are you and Mr. Panetta friends?" asked Ruthie.

"In a way," said Mr. Watkins. "We keep careful records here of the people who've purchased our puppies, and we stay in touch with them to make sure they're happy with their dogs. I'd rather take a dog back myself than have one mistreated."

"Wasn't Roland one of Dawn's puppies?" Kit asked.

"He was." Mr. Watkins shook his head regretfully. "In fact, *all* of the stolen dogs have been Dawn's puppies. The police believe someone who knows our kennel's reputation is tracking down Dawn's puppies and stealing them."

"I can see why you're upset," said Aunt Nancy. "I don't suppose you've been able to give the police any helpful leads?"

"I'm as baffled as they are," Mr. Watkins said. "Our kennel has a national reputation, and so does Dawn. The thief could be anyone involved in the show-dog world. But that's quite enough about the thefts. Shall we go see the puppies?"

Mr. Watkins led Aunt Nancy and the girls down a hallway and into a large, sunny room with ceiling fans whirring. The minute Mr. Watkins opened the door, five wide-eyed, wriggling puppies bounded forward, tripping over their long ears and oversize paws in their eagerness to greet Kit, Ruthie, and Aunt Nancy with their cool, sniffy noses and warm, pink tongues.

One puppy came right to Kit, wagging its tail

so vigorously, the puppy's entire back end was wagging, too. Kit laughed and stooped to pet the puppy. Then Kit spotted Dawn, the puppies' mother, resting in a wooden box in the corner of the room. Kit sucked in her breath. Dawn looked so much like Grace, the two dogs might have been twins. Dawn was black, brown, and white, just like Grace, with the same saddle-shaped marking on her back and the same white muzzle with freckles. For a moment all Kit could do was stare.

Mr. Watkins must have noticed. "She's a beautiful basset hound, isn't she?" he said to Kit.

"Yes, she is," Kit answered. "But the reason I was staring is that she looks so much like my dog, Grace."

"She does look like Grace!" exclaimed Ruthie.

"That's interesting," said Mr. Watkins. "If your basset looks so much like Dawn, Kit, chances are she's not as ordinary as you think. One of the reasons people pay so much attention to a dog's pedigree is that show dogs are judged according to the breed's standard—meaning how closely they resemble the ideal dog of the breed. Anyone who knows the breed's standard can tell at a glance if a dog is likely to be purebred.

"If your basset hound looks like Dawn, she must come from parents who were very close to the standard themselves. Where did you get her, Kit? A pet store?"

"No," Kit said. "I found her. Someone had abandoned her."

"Ah," said Mr. Watkins. "So many animals are being abandoned in these hard times. Believe it or not, one of Dawn's puppies was abandoned by the owner. At least we think she was. We call her our missing puppy, because we don't know what happened to her."

"Someone abandoned one of Dawn's pups?" asked Aunt Nancy. "That seems like throwing money out the window, since her puppies are worth so much."

"I don't think this woman knew what the puppy was worth," said Mr. Watkins. "She inherited the dog when her mother died. It was her mother, of course, who had purchased the dog as a puppy. When my trainer called to check up on the dog, the daughter said that she'd gotten rid of it, but she refused to say what she'd done with it.

Kit was struck with a sudden thought. Grace looked so much like Dawn—could she possibly be Dawn's missing puppy? Then Kit smiled at the unlikely idea. Grace was brave, but she wasn't very graceful, and she could be as stubborn as a mule. Kit just couldn't picture her prancing obediently around a show ring.

Besides, Kit thought, *right now it doesn't matter who Grace's parents were. All that matters is finding her.*

Mr. Watkins had started telling Aunt Nancy about the personality of each puppy, encouraging Aunt Nancy and the girls to pick up and hold any puppies they wanted to.

Kit swallowed. The puppies made her ache for Grace. Frustration gnawed at her, too. Their visit to the kennel was almost over, and they didn't know anything more about the Cadillac man than when they came. And it didn't seem there was any way to find out without flat-out asking Mr. Watkins who the man was—which they couldn't do.

Kit felt unsettled and restless. While Aunt Nancy and Ruthie cuddled the puppies, she wandered around the room, looking at the shelves and glass cases filled with trophies, ribbons, mementos, and photographs. The kennel's entire history seemed to be displayed in this room. Kit hoped she might be able to learn something that Mr. Watkins hadn't told them—something that might help in the search for Grace.

In one of the cabinets, a large framed photograph caught Kit's eye. It showed a younger Mr. Watkins with another man and a woman and a dog that looked like Dawn. They were standing in a grassy field where some cars were parked, and in the background a dog show was going on. Mr. Watkins had one arm around the woman—his wife, Kit guessed. The woman was holding a huge trophy. The other man was leaning against a fancy-looking car—a car with a hood ornament!

Was it a Cadillac? It was hard to tell. Only part of the car showed in the photograph.

Kit leaned closer to the cabinet, studying the photograph. Something in it seemed familiar. For a moment Kit couldn't figure out what it was. Then it struck her, and her heart began to pound.

The man leaning against the car was wearing a fedora with a feather in it.

10
A PROFITABLE SCHEME

Somehow Kit had to get Mr. Watkins to tell her who the man was, without arousing his suspicion. Kit turned around. Mr. Watkins was still showing puppies to Aunt Nancy and Ruthie. "Mr. Watkins," Kit asked, "is the dog in this photograph Dawn? It looks as if she's won a prize cup in an important dog show."

Mr. Watkins came over to the cabinet and stood beside Kit to look at the photograph. Aunt Nancy and Ruthie came, too. "Ah, yes," said Mr. Watkins. "That was the dog show in Indianapolis where Dawn won her championship title."

"Who are the other people in the picture?" asked Ruthie.

"That's my wife holding the cup," said

Mr. Watkins. "And our trainer, Norman Flint, leaning against the Cadillac."

It *was* a Cadillac! Kit, Ruthie, and Aunt Nancy looked quickly at one another.

Kit wanted to ask Mr. Watkins more about the car, but she couldn't think of a polite—and unsuspicious—way to do it. She shot Aunt Nancy a pleading glance.

Aunt Nancy gave Kit a tiny, almost imperceptible smile to show Kit she understood what Kit wanted. "Did you sell your Cadillac to your trainer?" Aunt Nancy asked Mr. Watkins.

"Gave it to him," said Mr. Watkins. "I felt bad about Flint losing his job when I closed the kennel. So I gave him the Cadillac and sold him the kennel's equipment dirt cheap. He always wanted to start his own kennel somewhere."

Norman Flint must be the Cadillac man! thought Kit. Frantically she tried to think of a way to keep Mr. Watkins talking about Flint. Maybe he would say something that would help them locate the man. "Your trainer is going to open a kennel of his own?" she asked.

"I don't know," said Mr. Watkins. "It was always a dream of his, but it takes money to start your own operation. In these times, money is hard to come by."

"Couldn't he use the equipment you sold him to start his own business?" asked Ruthie.

"It would give him a head start," said Mr. Watkins. "But opening a kennel can be very expensive. You have to buy a building, of course, purchase dogs to breed, hire a staff, and so much more. Flint is a resourceful man. If there's a way to raise the cash he needs for his kennel, Flint will find it."

Blood rushed through Kit's head. Was Norman Flint stealing valuable show dogs to finance his dream of starting his own kennel? Kit didn't understand how an ordinary pet like Grace could fit into such a scheme, but she had a feeling Flint was the key to finding Grace. Somehow she had to find out where Flint was now.

"Why didn't your trainer buy your building to open his kennel, Mr. Watkins?" Kit asked. "Isn't he going to stay in Cincinnati?"

"I don't think so," said Mr. Watkins. "The last time I saw Flint was when he came to clean out the building and take what he wanted. He said then he was planning to move to Canada as soon as he could."

Clean out the building and take what he wanted! An image flashed into Kit's mind of the empty file drawers in the deserted kennel. Flint must have taken whatever was in those drawers . . .

"When was that?" Aunt Nancy asked.

"A couple of months ago," Mr. Watkins answered a bit sadly. A shadow crossed his face. "I had hoped we'd stay in touch."

"Perhaps he's just been busy lately," Aunt Nancy said gently. She walked back over to the puppies. They were all in the box now with their mother, fast asleep. "I tell you, Mr. Watkins, every one of these puppies is so adorable, I can't make up my mind. Could I come again and bring my fiancé with me? He's much more decisive than I am."

"Why, certainly," said Mr. Watkins. "But come back soon. These puppies will go fast."

"I'll keep that in mind," said Aunt Nancy. After thanking Mr. Watkins, she whisked Kit and Ruthie out the door and back to her car.

As soon as they were in the car and on their way, Kit blurted out, "I've figured it out! Flint is the dog thief, and I know how he's been doing it!"

"I had the same impression—that Flint is your Cadillac man," said Aunt Nancy. "But you've figured out how he's pulling off the thefts, Kit?"

"How?" asked Ruthie.

"I think Flint took the kennel's records with him when he came to clean out the building," said Kit. "The file drawers are all empty. If he has the records, he would know who bought Dawn's puppies *and* where they lived."

"That's right," said Ruthie. "Mr. Watkins said they kept careful records on everyone who bought their puppies so that they could get in touch with them later."

"And those records would include names, addresses, and phone numbers," Aunt Nancy added. "Everything Flint would need to track down Dawn's puppies."

"He must be stealing Dawn's puppies so that he can sell them to make money to start his own kennel," said Kit.

"That *would* be a profitable scheme," said Aunt Nancy. She braked at a stop sign and checked for oncoming traffic. Then she started driving again. "There's a problem with that theory, though."

"What?" both Kit and Ruthie asked.

"We all heard Mr. Watkins," Aunt Nancy said. "When you sell a valuable pedigreed dog, you have to have registration papers. Since Flint is *stealing* the dogs, he won't have the registration papers, so he can't sell the dogs for what they're worth."

Kit and Ruthie were silent for a minute. Then Kit asked, in a tone that wasn't so confident, "But he could still sell the dogs, right? Just not for as *much* money as if they were show dogs?"

"I suppose so," said Aunt Nancy. "Somebody

would probably buy them, just because they're nice-looking dogs. But Flint would have to accept a much lower price for a dog without papers."

"I guess he'd have to steal twice as many dogs," said Ruthie.

"That could be his plan," agreed Aunt Nancy.

Kit was only half-listening. She was stuck on Aunt Nancy's words: *Somebody would probably buy them, just because they're nice-looking dogs.*

Kit's thoughts went hurtling backward, to the Sunday afternoon they were brainstorming about what might have happened to Grace. *If she was a particularly nice-looking dog,* Sergeant Paul had said, *a pet-store owner might be interested in buying her.*

Was Flint interested in Grace, too, Kit wondered, *for that very reason?*

The idea shook Kit up, because of what it would mean: that Flint might have stolen Grace in order to sell her to someone else!

Kit felt sick at the thought, but she forced herself to speak. "What if that *was* Flint's plan? And his plan included stealing Grace and trying to sell *her*? If Flint is the Cadillac man, he saw Grace in our yard when he drove by with the Muellers. Maybe he thought she looked like a dog that might be valuable."

Aunt Nancy was nodding. "I have to hand it to you, Kit. You've done some very good thinking. It all makes perfect sense." Nancy's eyes shone. "Wouldn't it be something if everything you girls have learned could help the police solve the dog-theft case—and find Grace at the same time?"

Kit and Ruthie gave each other an excited glance. "Aunt Nancy!" said Ruthie. "Can you tell Sergeant Paul about Flint right away? The police can arrest him, and Kit can get Grace back!"

"Wait a minute," said Aunt Nancy. "The police have to have facts and evidence before they can arrest anyone. I'll talk to Paul and tell him everything we've learned. Then the police can start investigating Flint—and the Muellers."

"But there's no time to wait for an *investigation!*" Kit protested. "By then Flint might

already have sold Grace. Or he might leave for
Canada and take Grace with him!"

"The police will work as quickly as they can,
Kit," said Aunt Nancy. "But they have to follow
the law."

"Then maybe we'll just have to find Grace
ourselves!" Ruthie burst out.

Abruptly Aunt Nancy pulled the car to the
side of the road, braked, and turned around to
face Kit and Ruthie in the backseat. "Ruthie,"
she said in a stern voice, "I absolutely forbid the
two of you to try to track down Flint. He could
be dangerous, and I don't want you girls to get
hurt. Do you understand me?"

Ruthie and Kit both said they understood.
Yet, inside, Kit was stewing. *How can I leave rescuing Grace up to strangers, even if they are the police?*

Then an idea occurred to her—a plan, really,
laid out in her mind as perfectly as a Monopoly
board—a plan to rescue Grace. And since Aunt
Nancy had said only that she forbade *the two of
them* to get involved in trying to find Flint, Kit
figured if she went *alone* to find him, without

Ruthie, she wouldn't be breaking her promise
to Aunt Nancy.

The next day Kit rushed through her
Saturday-morning chores. Mother had given
her permission to spend time looking for Grace,
and Kit was eager to set off and put her plan
into motion.

For her plan to work, she needed to be on
her own, so she didn't mind that Stirling wasn't
around. He was still working for his mother's
boss. The man had liked the job Stirling had
done for him so much, he had hired Stirling to
work for him every day until school started.

Kit had in mind to try to talk to the Mueller
boy—Sunny—alone, without his father around.
Since the Muellers had been helping Flint, Kit
figured they might know where to find him. She
didn't expect to get anything out of Mr. Mueller,
but Sunny might be different. It was Sunny who
had let her into their house. Maybe he'd felt

sorry for her. Maybe he would tell her where Flint lived. Somehow Kit had to get Sunny alone to talk to him, but she wasn't sure just how she would do it.

On the long walk to the Muellers', Kit thought about it, but she still hadn't come up with anything when she reached Riverview Lane. From the corner, she could see the Muellers' house perched on the embankment, and she spied Mr. Mueller leaning against a railing on the front porch, smoking a pipe. He wasn't looking down toward the street but was staring out toward the trees that lined the river, as if he was lost in thought.

Suddenly an idea came to Kit. *If I can get to the Muellers' back door without Mr. Mueller seeing me, maybe I can get Sunny to come outside and talk to me.* The thought of knocking on the Muellers' door again made Kit's throat dry with dread. *But for Grace, I can do it,* Kit thought.

Quickly she glanced around. The bald man's Model T wasn't parked in his yard, which probably meant he wasn't home. She took a deep breath and pitched herself up the hill through the bald man's yard, running as fast as she could. Around his house she went, across his muddy, trash-strewn backyard and through the tiny backyard next to his.

Then she stopped, panting, sweat trickling down her face. One house over was the Muellers'. Sunny was out back, his mouth full of clothes-pins, hanging diapers on the line. Relief flooded Kit. She sprinted across the last yard toward him. Sunny was bent over, pulling a wet diaper out of a wicker basket. When he looked up and saw her, he gave a little jump. She heard the sharp intake of his breath.

"I need to talk to you," she said.

He straightened and took the clothespins out of his mouth. "What about?" His voice shook, and Kit noticed that his knees were quivering.

"About my dog, Grace. The dog *you* took." Kit stepped toward Sunny. "I know about Flint, and I know you and your father have been help-ing him steal dogs, including Grace. The police will be after Flint soon, and they'll be after you, too, unless you tell me where Grace is."

Sunny's face went as white as the diapers on the line. "We can't talk here. Across the street, near the riverbank, there's a boulder in a grove of willows. Wait for me there, behind the boulder. I'll get away as soon as I can."

From the house, a woman's voice called, "Luke! Luke!" followed by some question in German that Kit didn't understand.

"Go!" Sunny said in an urgent whisper. *"Please."*

Kit gave a nod and darted away, into the yard next door. Behind her, she heard Sunny say, "It's no one, Mother. I'm talking to myself."

Kit ran back around the bald man's house and down the hill, pausing only long enough to glance over her shoulder at Mr. Mueller, still smoking his pipe. Kit shot across the street and into the wooded area along the riverbank. She spotted the boulder and ducked behind it. Then she leaned against the stone and tried to catch her breath. A slight breeze blew off the river and cooled Kit's sweaty face.

Endless minutes passed. Kit watched a tugboat on the river, slowly pulling a barge loaded with coal. She swatted a mosquito that landed on her arm. *Where is Sunny?* she wondered. *Was it a trick telling me to come here?*

Then she heard twigs snap, and Sunny came around the boulder. He stood stiffly, facing her, lines of tension at the corners of his mouth. "How did you find us?" he asked. "Did the hoboes tell you? You must have been to the jungle, since you called me Sunny."

Kit nodded. "I didn't know your real name." He waited expectantly, but Kit clammed up. She wanted *him* to do the talking.

"My name is Luke," he said, "though I don't mind being called Sunny. The hoboes meant the name kindly, and I've gotten used to it."

Kit thrust out her chin. "Luke—Sunny— whoever you are—tell me where Grace is. I want her *back*."

"I don't *know* where she is." Luke ran a hand through his shaggy blond hair. "Flint took her. I wish I *could* give her back to you and undo everything that's happened." He looked at Kit with troubled eyes, and she was shocked to see them glistening with tears. "I hate Flint!" he said. "I wish Papa had never met him!"

"If you hate Flint so much," Kit said in a softer tone, "why did you and your father agree to help him?"

"We didn't *agree*," said Luke. "Flint *tricked* us. He told Papa he had a job for him, but he didn't tell us what the job was."

Flint had paid his father in advance, Luke told her, and Mr. Mueller had spent the money on things they desperately needed. Only then had Flint informed Mr. Mueller that the job he had for him was stealing dogs— and that Luke would have to help. In fact, Luke would have to do the first job himself—stealing a basset hound Flint had read about in the newspaper.

"So that's how Flint found Grace!" Kit said.

Luke went on. "Flint threatened to have Papa arrested if I didn't do the job, unless Papa gave him back his money. He knew Papa had spent it, so he knew he had us trapped." His thin shoulders sagged. "After I stole your dog, Papa and I thought that would be the end of it. But Flint had different ideas. He's threatening to turn us in to the police unless we steal another dog for him."

"So you're helping Flint steal another basset hound," Kit said. Almost to herself she added, "Another show dog. Another of Dawn's puppies."

"No!" Luke's face flamed. "We haven't yet—" Then he looked at her sharply. "Did you say *Dawn's puppies*?"

"Yes," said Kit. "What about it?"

"Flint showed Papa and me a newspaper clipping about your dog saving your family from a fire. On the clipping was a picture of you with your dog, and Flint had written *Dawn's puppy* across it, with a question mark after it."

Kit recalled Mr. Watkins' words: *One of Dawn's puppies was abandoned ... we call her our missing puppy.*

Kit started breathing fast. Did Flint actually think Grace *was* Dawn's missing puppy?

11
PERFECT HIDEOUT

The idea seemed far-fetched to Kit. Yes, Grace looked a lot like Dawn, but she was just an ordinary basset hound, not a dog with registration papers and a pedigree. Then an image sprang into Kit's mind—a line she'd written in her notebook: Unknown where Grace was born.

Kit's mouth fell open. If Flint believed Grace was Shy-Anne Kennel's missing puppy— or even if he just thought he could pass Grace off as Dawn's puppy—it would explain so much. Grace could be as valuable to him as one of the show dogs. And those dogs were worth hundreds of dollars—maybe more. Flint must have thought he could sell *Grace* for hundreds of dollars, too!

Cold horror spread over Kit. Somehow she

had to get Grace back before Flint sold her. Through the panic clouding her brain, Kit forced herself to think.

There might be a way...

"Listen," she said to Luke. "I've got a plan, and I need you to help me."

Luke was already shaking his head. "I'd like to help you... I really would... but I can't. You don't understand how Flint has us trapped. If we don't do what he wants, he'll have us arrested. If Papa and I go to jail, there'll be no one to look after my mother and the baby—"

"Just hear me out," Kit interrupted. "There's a way out for you and your father, too. If you tell me where Flint lives, the two of us can go there and steal Grace *back*. Then you won't have to worry about Flint's threats. If I have Grace back, I'll just claim that she was never stolen. You and your father will be free. The police are already investigating the dog thefts, and before long they'll arrest Flint—"

"'Before long' will be too late for us!" Luke exclaimed.

"What do you mean?"

"Flint wants Papa to steal a dog that's coming to the Labor Day Dog Show on Monday. Papa's supposed to put the stolen dog in Flint's car, and Flint said he'll be watching from the audience to make sure Papa does it. If Papa doesn't cooperate, Flint threatened to have us arrested for stealing the money he gave Papa."

"But you didn't steal that money," Kit said. "Flint *gave* it to you."

Luke shrugged. "It would be our word against his, and who would believe *us*—a couple of poor hoboes? Not the police. The police don't trust hoboes."

Kit's thoughts flew. "If you're willing to help me try to get Grace back," she told Luke, "I can help you, too. I have a friend who's a police sergeant. He knows the officers who've been working on the dog-theft case. If we go to Sergeant Paul and tell him everything, I know he'll do what he can for you and your father."

Luke hesitated only a moment before

agreeing to help Kit. "What do we need to do?" he asked her.

"We'll go to Flint's house and see if he has Grace. You know where he lives, right?"

"No," said Luke. "Flint did his best not to let us know too much about him. I don't even know his first name."

As quick as the snap of a finger, a series of thoughts shot through Kit's head. *Flint's first name... Butch's last name... pages of Johnsons in the phone book—*

The phone book! Kit felt stupid for not thinking of it before. "*I* know Flint's first name," she said. "If he lives here in Cincinnati, I can look up his address in the phone book."

"I'm pretty sure he does," said Luke. "What'll we do once we find out whether Grace is at his house?"

"I hope she'll be outside, in a pen or in his yard. Then we'll just take her. If she's not outside... well, then we'll have to figure out what to do next."

"You know the risk we're taking, don't you?"

said Luke. "If Flint catches us sneaking around his yard—"

"He won't catch us," said Kit. *I hope,* she added silently.

The next day was Sunday. Kit met Luke at Mount Storm Park after lunch, and they headed to Flint's house, in a neighborhood called Greendale Heights near downtown. In the early-September heat, the walk seemed endless. The sun beat down on them, and the air above the pavement shimmered with waves of heat. Sweat trickled down Kit's face and made her clothes cling to her body as if they were fastened with glue.

Once they were in Flint's neighborhood, the air felt cooler. Big trees shaded the street, and a hot wind stirred the leaves overhead. Flint's house was on a dead-end street. Large, overgrown shrubs surrounded the house and secluded it from the other homes.

The house was built on a hill, and the yard sloped down to an exposed basement in back. A chain-link fence overgrown with vines enclosed the backyard. In front of the house was a gravel driveway, but there was no Cadillac in sight.

"Jeepers," Kit said. "What a perfect place to hide stolen dogs from nosy neighbors."

"Yeah," said Luke. "And we're in luck. It doesn't look like he's home."

"Come on," Kit said, "let's take a look in the backyard."

They went around the side of the house, taking care on the sloping ground. Over the fence Kit could see dog pens in the backyard—all empty. Kit rushed through the gate, with Luke at her heels. Together they checked the pens. Water dishes were still full, and flies buzzed above crumbs left in the food bowls. A few well-chewed bones and some dog toys were scattered about.

"Look!" Luke pointed to a blue rubber bone in one of the pens. "That's the toy Papa bought for Grace! I gave it to Flint when he took her."

"Then Grace *was* here." Kit reached into the pen and picked up the rubber bone. Kit felt an ache inside. How long ago had Grace been gnawing on this toy? "What's Flint *done* with her? And where are the other dogs?"

"Maybe he sold them already," said Luke.

"No!" A sob caught in Kit's throat. "He *couldn't* have sold Grace." Deep down, Kit knew it was possible, but she wouldn't let herself believe it. "He couldn't have sold so many stolen dogs so fast. Maybe he moved them into the house to keep the neighbors from getting suspicious."

"Could be," said Luke. "I'll sneak around to the side of the house and try to look in the windows."

"I'll look in the basement," said Kit.

Luke nodded. In a minute he had disappeared around the side of the house. Kit went to the basement and peered through an open window.

Inside, a fan whirred. Opened boxes of files sat about the room, with more files stacked on a

table below the window. Next to the table was a
desk with a typewriter and a telephone. Papers
were strewn on the desk, their edges gently
stirred by the air from the fan.

For a moment Kit stared at the papers.
They seemed familiar. Where had she seen them
before?

She had to get a closer look. In a few steps,
Kit was at the basement door, hoping it wasn't
locked. She turned the knob and pushed. The
door opened! Kit edged into the room, her heart
thudding. She leaned toward the desk to inspect
the papers. Now she knew where she'd seen
something like them before: at Shy-Anne Kennel.
They were dog registration papers, like the ones
showing Dawn's pedigree.

But these papers weren't *exactly* like Dawn's.
Some of the pedigree papers were blank, with
nothing printed in the spaces where the owner's
name and the dog's parents' names should have
been. Some papers were partially filled in, and
others were completed. A partially filled-in
paper was still in the typewriter, as if someone

had been interrupted in the middle of typing information on it.

Kit struggled a minute to make sense of what she was seeing. It looked as if Flint was in the process of creating registration papers. But Kit remembered Mr. Watkins saying that only the *AKC* could issue registration papers.

Kit stepped closer and bent over the desk to read the pedigree information Flint had typed on one of the finished documents. Her breath caught. The dog's name on the form was Roland Red Sky Delight—which had to be Mr. Panetta's dog, Roland—but *Flint* was listed as the owner. Flint was making false registration papers!

Quickly Kit rifled through the other forms. On every form, Flint had typed his own name in the space for the owner.

Now Kit understood Flint's scheme: instead of accepting a lower price for the show dogs than what they were worth, Flint was pretending he was the legitimate owner with legitimate registration papers. That way, he could sell the dogs for hundreds, maybe even thousands, of dollars. That would give Flint plenty of money to start his own kennel.

At that moment Luke appeared in the door-way. "Kit! Flint's coming!" Then Kit heard the sound of a car engine and tires crunching over gravel.

"Quick!" Kit cried. "Hide in the bushes!" She raced through the door, pulling it shut behind her. Luke was already heading for the shrubs nearby, and Kit was right behind him.

They dived behind the bushes just as Flint came walking down the hill. Kit could see him through gaps in the foliage. Flint opened the gate, walked across the yard, and opened the basement door. Then he went inside. Kit heard the fan cut off. She moved closer and pulled branches aside so that she could peek through and see Flint. He was standing at the window, dialing the telephone.

Kit strained to hear Flint's end of the conversation. "Flint here," he said. A pause. "That's right. You'll be impressed with her. She's tricolored—a real beauty—and a daughter of

Walhampton Day-Dawn. No show experience yet, but an excellent pedigree."

Kit's stomach lurched. *Flint must be talking about Grace.* As far as Kit knew, Grace was the only stolen dog that wasn't a show dog.

"You'll be available when?" Flint paused, listening to the voice on the other end of the line. Then he said, "Yes, I'll have her papers with me. You bring the money. Cash." Pause. "No, not here. I'm ... ahh ... having to move out unexpectedly. Is there somewhere else—" Pause. "Fine, that'll work. I'll see you then."

It sounded as if Flint was setting up a meeting to sell Grace! But when? And where? And to whom? If only Flint would say more.

Then came the *thunk* of Flint hanging up the phone, and Kit's stomach dropped, too. *Gracie, oh Gracie,* Kit thought. *How will I get you back **now**?*

Tears stung Kit's eyes. Beside her, she heard Luke's tense breathing. She saw Flint moving around the room, stooping and bending, as if he was closing up boxes. Then he came back to the desk, set a box down, and started packing things in it: first the typewriter, then some files from the table, and last, the registration papers.

After he closed the box, he picked it up and went out. For a moment he stood in the open doorway, looking back into the room. "I guess I've got everything important," he muttered. "The movers can get the rest." Then he shut the door, locked it, and trudged across the yard, through the gate, and up the hill.

Kit's eyes met Luke's. "Is he gone?" Luke whispered.

Kit nodded. She was too stunned from what she'd seen and heard to talk. Then came the slam of a car door, the growl of the engine starting, and the crunching of tires on gravel. At last the sound of the engine faded away.

Kit and Luke stumbled out of the bushes. Kit felt weak-kneed and shaky.

"Did you hear Flint?" Luke asked. "What do you make of it?"

Kit's throat felt as dry as cotton. "Sounds like he's planning to sell Grace," she croaked.

"Yeah. *And* it sounds like he's decided to take the dogs and move somewhere else—in a big hurry. I wonder why."

"Maybe he thinks the police are about to catch up with him," said Kit.

A stricken look crossed Luke's face. "Then maybe the police are about to catch up with Papa and me, too. What are we going to do, Kit?"

"I don't know," said Kit. "I have to think." She struggled to push down the panic rising inside her—the fear that Flint would sell Grace, and Kit would never see her again. For all they knew, Flint would be in town only until tomorrow—Labor Day—when he'd planned to meet Luke and his father at the dog show to pick up the dog he wanted them to steal.

Time to find Grace was running out fast.

12
ORDINARY HOUND

Suddenly Aunt Nancy's words jumped into Kit's mind: *The police have to have facts and evidence before they can arrest anyone...*

Kit turned quickly to Luke. "If we tell Sergeant Paul what we've seen here, it might give the police enough evidence to arrest Flint before he can sell Grace. Sergeant Paul's been working almost every weekend. If we go now to the police station, maybe he'll be there. We can talk to him about helping you and your father, too."

"It's worth a try," agreed Luke.

Kit barely spoke on the walk to the station with Luke. All the way, she was hoping and praying that Sergeant Paul would be there and worrying about what she would do if he wasn't.

When the officer at the front desk said Sergeant Paul had just come in from patrol, Kit felt a rush of relief.

Sergeant Paul sat at his desk and listened intently while Kit and Luke told him all they'd found out about Flint. They explained how Flint had blackmailed the Muellers into helping him and that another theft was planned for the Labor Day Dog Show.

When they'd finished, Sergeant Paul drew a careful breath. "It would be perfect if we could catch Flint in the act of stealing a dog," he said. "Think your dad would be willing to help us catch him at the dog show, Luke? We'd have him pretend to make the theft as planned, but we'd be there to arrest Flint as soon as he takes possession of the dog. It's called a police sting operation. We'd be awfully grateful to your dad if he'd help."

Luke was sure his father would agree.

"What can *I* do to help?" asked Kit.

"You've already helped us track down Flint," said Sergeant Paul. "That's quite enough. We'll try to get Grace back for you, too. I wish I could promise that we will, Kit, but you know I can't."

Kit gulped back a sob and nodded.

The next day was Labor Day—the day of the dog show. By the time Kit and Ruthie got to the fairgrounds, the show had already begun. Roped-off areas in the middle of the fairgrounds served as rings. Inside the rings, dogs were competing, running or trotting on leashes beside their handlers or standing still to be judged. Clustered around the rings were tents where dogs were being groomed and readied to compete. Souvenir and food stands were strung out along one edge of the fairgrounds. Behind the food stands was the parking area.

People and dogs were everywhere. Spectators were sitting in folding chairs or standing around the rings. Other people were browsing for souvenirs or eating at tables set up near the food stands. Trainers, dog handlers, and owners led their dogs to and from the rings and exercised them in special areas.

All around were dogs of every breed, shape, and size. There were Labradors and Dalmatians, poodles and Pekinese, spaniels, terriers, boxers, and basset hounds. Every dog was well behaved, with perfect looks and perfect manners. The dogs had been washed and fluffed, combed and trimmed. Their hair had ribbons and curls; their coats were clean and shiny. Not a single dog was pulling at its leash, or jumping up on people, or trying to run away from its owner.

How Kit longed for good old imperfect Grace!

Among the crowd, lots of men were wearing fedoras. Kit couldn't help glancing at all their faces, wondering if she'd even recognize Flint if she saw him up close.

Ruthie gave Kit a sympathetic look. "You know, Kit," she said, "Flint might not be wearing his fedora today. And besides, we're not supposed to be *looking* for him. Sergeant Paul warned us not to do anything that might make Flint suspicious, remember?"

"I'm not really looking for Flint—just *thinking* about him," said Kit, "and about Grace. I keep worrying that Flint might have already sold her. If the police catch Flint here at the show, but he doesn't have Grace anymore, everything we've done will have been for nothing."

Ruthie put a sympathetic hand on Kit's shoulder. "We just have to keep hoping," she said. She gave Kit an encouraging hug. "Come on, let's get some lunch."

Ruthie pointed to one of the food stands, and the girls joined the winding line. They had to wait a long time, but finally Kit had her hot dog and potato chips. While Ruthie was ordering her food, Kit went over to the condiment booth to put mustard and relish on her hot dog.

Nearby was the parking area, lined with cars and trucks. Near their cars, people had set up pens where their dogs could rest when they weren't competing in the show. In one pen, a huge Great Dane was playing gently with a tiny

Chihuahua. It made Kit ache all the more for her own playful Grace.

Then Kit noticed two men talking near the cotton-candy stand some distance away. One of the men had a basset hound on a leash, and the dog was acting up. The man was trying to get it to stand a certain way and to hold its head a certain way, but the basset hound wasn't cooperating. It wouldn't stand still, and it wouldn't keep its head still. It kept trying to jerk its head away from the man's grasp.

Finally the dog managed for one brief instant to turn its head, and it looked in Kit's direction. Kit's heart leaped into her throat. The dog was Grace!

Was Flint trying to sell Grace to the other man?

"What are you staring at, Kit?" Ruthie asked, coming over to the condiment booth with her hot dog.

Kit pointed. "Over there! It's Flint. And he's got Grace with him! I think he's trying to sell her."

"We can't let him sell Grace!" said Ruthie.

"I know! We've got to stop him somehow." Frantically Kit looked around for Sergeant Paul. But there was no policeman in sight. *Has the sting operation been called off?* she wondered. If so, Flint might never be caught—and she might never see Grace again!

Then Kit saw Flint reach into the pocket of his jacket, pull out some folded papers, and hand them to the other man. *The false registration papers...*

An idea slammed into Kit's brain. "Ruthie!" Kit said. "We can tell Flint's buyer that Grace belongs to me and that she's nothing but an ordinary dog! When he knows she doesn't have a pedigree, he won't want her anymore."

"That doesn't mean Flint will hand Grace over to *us*," said Ruthie. "And he'll be angry. No telling what he might do." Ruthie's eyes were wide and scared.

"It's our only chance to get Grace back," said Kit. "We have to *try*."

For a few seconds, Ruthie looked worried.

Then she said, "Okay, let's go."

The girls left their food at the booth and hurried toward the cotton-candy stand. Just as they did, judging in one of the rings ended, and spectators began pouring out of their seats into the walkway. Kit and Ruthie could barely make their way through the press of people milling around. "We'll never make it in time to stop Flint!" said Kit.

Then a security guard came and began redirecting people, so the crowd began to thin. Kit could see the cotton-candy stand. Flint and the buyer were still there—and so was Grace!

"Come on!" Kit said to Ruthie. They broke into a jog, dodging around the people in front of them.

Then Grace spotted Kit. Grace went wild, jumping and wagging her tail, barking, pulling hard at the leash, trying to get away from Flint. People all around were gawking. The security guard was staring, and Flint's buyer looked surprised and upset. Flint was struggling to get Grace under control, yanking on the leash again and again, but Grace kept trying harder to bound toward Kit.

Kit and Ruthie came running up to Flint. "Stop it!" said Kit. "You're hurting her!"

At the sound of Kit's voice, Grace lunged forward, barking joyously, but Flint jerked her back. "I'll thank you girls to move away from my dog. You're causing a disruption."

"She's *my* dog," Kit exclaimed, "and you know it!"

"I don't know what you're talking about," Flint said. "This animal belongs to me. I'm about to sell her, and you're interfering. Move along, please, before I call a security guard."

Now Flint's buyer was frowning. "What is this about, Mr. Flint? Who are these girls?"

"I don't know *who* they are," said Flint. "But I'm going to take care of them right now." He looked around until his gaze locked on the security guard. "Excuse me a minute, Mr. Amos," he said to the buyer.

Flint strode toward the security guard, dragging Grace with him. Grace was doing her best not to go, but she couldn't help being pulled along. Kit and Ruthie hurried after Flint.

When Kit saw Flint smile and shake hands with the guard, her stomach clenched. The two of them must be friends.

"Mr. Flint," the guard said heartily. "It's good to see you again. What seems to be the problem here?"

"These girls have cooked up some scheme to steal my basset hound by claiming it's theirs," said Flint. "If you'll escort them out, I won't press charges against them."

Kit couldn't believe it. *Flint was claiming they were trying to steal Grace from **him**!* "Grace is mine," Kit said fiercely. *"He took her from me!"*

Hearing Kit, Grace *woofed* and made a move toward her. Flint, with a flick of his wrist, pulled the leash tighter, and Grace had to stop.

He smiled at Kit in a patronizing way. "What did I tell you, Harvey? Their story is so outrageous, it's almost funny."

"It's not a story!" Ruthie exclaimed. "It's the truth! Look! See how much Grace loves Kit.

She's dying to get to her. But Grace doesn't like *him* at all." Ruthie pointed to Flint. "If you won't believe us, believe *Grace*."

The guard looked a bit befuddled. "Well, the dog sure does seem to like you girls—"

"Oh, please," said Flint in a tone of strained patience. The *please* came out like *puh-leez*. "Basset hounds love everyone. They're the friendliest dogs alive. Listen, Harvey, I can settle this once and for all. I'm about to sell the dog, and I've given her registration papers to my friend Mr. Amos over there." He nodded toward the buyer over at the concession stand. "If you'd like, I can go get her papers and show them to you."

The guard held his arms in front of him, palms out. "That's not necessary, Mr. Flint. I've worked enough dog shows to know your impeccable reputation."

"He's lying!" Kit said. "The papers he has are false!"

But the guard cut her off. "Girls, I'm going to have to ask you to come with me. We'll find your parents, and if they're not here, we'll call them to come pick you up." He gave Flint a nod. "Mr. Flint, please take your dog and enjoy the rest of the show."

Kit blinked in disbelief. The guard was giving Grace to Flint!

"I'm leaving after I make this sale," Flint told the guard. "I've bought some new dogs, and I'm heading out of town with them now. I'm leaving Cincinnati, Harvey. Starting up my own operation in Canada."

"Good luck with it then," said the guard.

Then the guard stepped toward Kit and Ruthie and put a hand on each of their shoulders. At the same time, Flint began trying to walk away with Grace, but Grace wouldn't budge, no matter how much Flint jerked on the leash. Grace whimpered and strained toward Kit.

With an angry expression, Flint bent down, heaved Grace up, and started off with her. Grace wriggled, but Flint held her tight, though he seemed to stagger a bit under her weight. Grace stared at Kit over Flint's shoulder, her big brown eyes seeming to beg Kit to rescue her.

A sob came up in Kit's throat. She couldn't go after Flint because the guard was grasping her shoulder. She would have to make Grace come to her...

"Come, Gracie, come!" Kit called. "Come to Kit!"

After that, things happened at lightning speed. Grace struggled free from Flint and leaped from his grasp. Flint, thrown off balance, stumbled and dropped the leash. Grace, her leash trailing behind, charged toward Kit. Kit and Ruthie broke away from the guard and ran toward Grace. Girls and dog met in a burst of hugging and licking, kissing and tail wagging. Kit and Ruthie wrapped their arms around Grace. The security guard came hurrying toward Kit and Ruthie from one direction, and Flint came from the other.

Then Kit glimpsed Sergeant Paul and another officer coming through the crowd. Flint must have seen them, too. He turned and made a sudden dash toward the parking area under the trees, where he must have parked his car. The officer sprinted after Flint, dodging around people, who tried to get out of the two men's way.

Flint had almost reached the parking area when a police car came screaming up, lights flashing. The car screeched to a stop and two more policemen jumped out. Flint stopped and held his arms in the air as the policemen surrounded him and put him under arrest.

Sergeant Paul had stayed with Kit and Ruthie. Everywhere nearby, dogs were howling and barking at the sirens. People were staring and pointing, talking loudly, and crowding around Sergeant Paul to ask him what was happening. The entire scene was chaos and confusion.

But Grace ignored everything except Kit and Ruthie. The girls were kneeling beside her. Grace was licking them all over, her tail swishing merrily. Happy tears streamed down Kit's face, and Ruthie couldn't stop giggling.

When the police car at last drove off with

Flint, Sergeant Paul managed to calm people down. All the dogs settled down too, and everyone turned their attention back to the dog show. Sergeant Paul walked over to the girls.

Kit and Ruthie were sitting on the ground, and Grace was stretched out on her back across their laps. They were scratching her belly, and Grace's mouth was wide open in a doggie grin. Sergeant Paul knelt beside the girls and scratched Grace, too. "She's happy as a clam, isn't she?" he said.

"She's happy to be back with Kit," said Ruthie.

"We thought you'd be angry with us," Kit said.

"Because we wrecked your sting operation by going after Grace," Ruthie added.

Sergeant Paul smiled. "Thanks to your detective work, we didn't need the sting operation. Grace was a stolen dog, too, and finding Flint with her was all the proof we needed to arrest him. If Grace hadn't gone missing, it might've taken us much longer to solve this case."

"I guess that makes Grace a hero all over again," said Ruthie.

"I guess it does," said Sergeant Paul with a laugh.

"Hey, Kit," said Ruthie, "you can write another article about her. She'll be an even bigger celebrity than before—"

"Oh, no," Kit interrupted. "Grace is retiring from the celebrity business *forever*. From now on, she's going to be plain old ordinary *Grace*."

LOOKING BACK

A PEEK INTO THE PAST

Many people in Kit's time faced terrible poverty.

During the Great Depression, life was very hard for many families—and for their pets, too. Many people sadly realized that they simply could not afford to keep their pets anymore. Across the country, thousands of dogs and cats were abandoned.

Just as hoboes traveled from place to place seeking work and food, abandoned animals roamed neighborhoods looking for scraps of food. When Kit first found Grace, the dog was wet, hungry, and all alone. A handwritten note tied around her neck said, "Can't feed her any more." Kit took Grace home, and the Kittredges adopted her. But many stray animals were not so lucky.

One woman who grew up during Kit's time recalled that her family refused to feed stray dogs and cats. Her grandmother said that there wasn't enough food for people, much less for animals. So every day on her way to school, the girl left her lunch in the bushes for starving strays to eat. She would watch them devour every bite, even the wax paper. These sad memories made such an impression on her that when she grew up, she started an organization to care for abandoned animals.

Yet even people who couldn't afford to own dogs seemed eager to hear about them. In the 1930s, movies featuring a German shepherd named Rin Tin Tin were hugely popular, and Americans loved to read about glamorous Hollywood movie stars and their elegant dogs.

A German shepherd was a famous movie star in the 1930s.

Trainers get their poodles ready for judging at a 1930s dog show.

Local dog shows, like the one Kit attends in the mystery, provided entertainment for people worn down by the Depression. The crowds who attended had fun just looking at the different breeds and watching proud owners and trainers walk their dogs around the show ring. One boy who attended a Cincinnati dog show in 1935 saw a young beagle win a prize. "All the way home," he later wrote, "all Dad and I could talk about was this wonderful little dog."

To compete in a show, a dog must have registration papers proving that it is *purebred*—that the dog's parents belonged to only one breed, with no other breed mixed in. Grace's papers, for example, would have shown that she was pure basset hound.

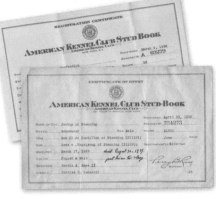

Registration papers *provide important details about a purebred dog's birth and breeding.*

At a show, dogs compete against other males or females of the same breed. A judge examines each dog to see how well it matches the *standard*, or the ideal characteristics, for its breed. Judges check the dog's size,

A judge examines how well this basset hound matches the ideal traits for its breed—such as droopy jowls, dangling ears, smooth coat, long back, deep chest, and short, sturdy legs.

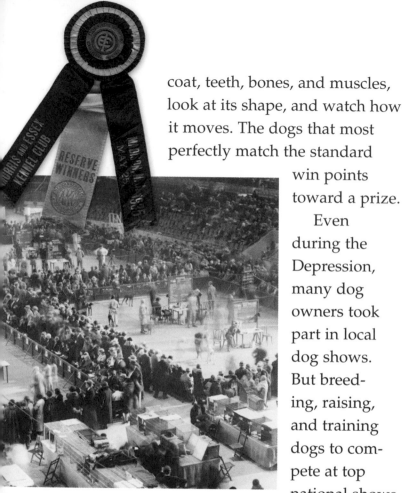

coat, teeth, bones, and muscles, look at its shape, and watch how it moves. The dogs that most perfectly match the standard win points toward a prize.

Even during the Depression, many dog owners took part in local dog shows. But breed-ing, raising, and training dogs to com-pete at top national shows takes a lot of money and time. In the 1930s, that was mostly a hobby of the wealthy. Dog shows such as the yearly

National champions are selected at the Westminster Dog Show, seen here in the 1930s.

Trainer John G. Bates and his champion terrier, Blarney's Bit o' Luck, made the cover of Time *magazine in 1938.*

Westminster Dog Show in New York City were high-society events that drew the rich and famous. Ordinary people across the country were so interested in these shows that winning trainers and their dogs even appeared on the covers of major news magazines!

However, during the Depression most pets weren't show animals or champions. They were simply regular dogs and cats who brought comfort, fun, and happiness to the people who loved them—just like pets today.

About the Author

Elizabeth McDavid Jones has lived most of her life in North Carolina. Her earliest passions were animals and writing. As a girl, she especially loved to write stories about animals.

Today, she lives in Virginia with her husband and children. She is the author of three mysteries about Felicity Merriman: *Peril at King's Creek, Traitor in Williamsburg,* and *Lady Margaret's Ghost.*

She also wrote five American Girl History Mysteries: *The Night Flyers,* which won the Edgar Allan Poe Award for Best Children's Mystery; *Secrets on 26th Street; Watcher in the Piney Woods; Mystery on Skull Island;* and *Ghost Light on Graveyard Shoal,* an Agatha Award nominee for Best Children's/Young Adult Mystery.